CROSSING THE BRIDGE

CROSSING THE BRIDGE

BERNARD THOROGOOD

Copyright © 2015 by Bernard Thorogood.

Library of Congress Control Number:		2015914416
ISBN:	Hardcover	978-1-5035-0977-1
	Softcover	978-1-5035-0978-8
	eBook	978-1-5035-0979-5

All rights reserved. No part of this book may be reproduced or transmitted in any form or by any means, electronic or mechanical, including photocopying, recording, or by any information storage and retrieval system, without permission in writing from the copyright owner.

This is a work of fiction. Names, characters, places and incidents either are the product of the author's imagination or are used fictitiously, and any resemblance to any actual persons, living or dead, events, or locales is entirely coincidental.

Any people depicted in stock imagery provided by Thinkstock are models, and such images are being used for illustrative purposes only.
Certain stock imagery © Thinkstock.

Print information available on the last page.

Rev. date: 09/02/2015

To order additional copies of this book, contact:
Xlibris
1-800-455-039
www.Xlibris.com.au
Orders@Xlibris.com.au
720723

After the walled enclosure of the Moscow Patriarchate, Niki had found Geneva to be a liberating, stimulating experience. He had come as the Russian Orthodox representative to work with the World Council of Churches at its headquarters, not far from the airport, and looking south towards the distant peaks around Mont Blanc. The mountains were normally hidden by cloud or drizzle, but visitors were always assured that the view was very fine. Niki, whose full name was Nikolas Demenchov, was thirty two, a deacon, well read, his beard neatly trimmed, his student expertise was in historical theology. His wife Petrovna was an infant teacher, able to do some part-time work in the child-care centre. They had no children. Niki stood very upright so that he looked taller than he really was. He spoke good English and better French. With a smiling openness, he readily made friends.

Niki's assignment was to help staff the Faith and Order division of the Council which was always short of funds. Since the Patriarchate was paying his stipend, he was doubly welcome. The Faith and Order programme was dedicated to continue the work which developed from the early 20th century to heal the divisions between the Christian churches, a slow and erratic progress seeking to reverse the long separations and anathemas and so to present a more truly reconciled body to the world. There were, in the 1970s, some flash points of disunity. In Eastern Europe enthusiastic Catholics were challenging the monopoly of the Orthodox, with community disturbance and some local violence. In Latin America there were growing outbursts of Pentecostal fervour among the favelas which shook the complacency of the Catholic hierarchy. In Ireland the civil unrest and the violence in the North set the Catholics and Protestants facing each other across barbed wire.

The longer-term work was to seek the maximum agreement of the churches to the basics of Christian life and witness. This meant keeping conversations going for years. Propositions were always taken home to church authorities which then consulted, listened to their theologians, prepared responses and so fed the next round of meetings – a slow process which suggested that there was little urgency in the cause. Niki soon found himself wrapped up in the process, seeking to explain the Orthodox position and its basis in ancient tradition. He was among Protestants. They formed the great majority of the member churches. It was people from their denominational staffs who were usually seconded to work in Geneva, and generally they were very ignorant of the Orthodox theology and tradition.

Where were the Catholics? They kept apart. They could not bring themselves to be just one church among all the others, since they were sure that only they were the true church of God. It was an alarming self-esteem, but carried with much learning and, it must be acknowledged, with many examples of holiness. In the Vatican the engagement in ecumenism was entrusted to the Secretariat for Christian Unity, headed by Cardinal Terracini. There was a Joint Committee at which the Secretariat and the WCC were able to discuss the many issues prohibiting unity, and Niki found himself regularly sitting in this group, gaining insight into the moods and hopes of both sides.

At one meeting they were tackling the issue of inter-faith marriage and the Catholic insistence that before the wedding the couple should promise that any children of the marriage would be brought up as Catholics; this was a condition for a priest to officiate at the wedding.

"But don't you see that this is very one-sided and unfair?"

"It has always been the discipline of the Church and ensures that the children will have a Christian upbringing."

"The other partner surely has rights too. Why should a convinced Methodist or Anglican have to give way every time? Isn't that hurtful?"

"We seek some stability, some assurance or it is likely that there will be a serious drift into secularism, and no religious teaching at all."

"Yes, Nicholas, what are you suggesting?"

"It seems to me that we all want to ensure as far as we can that children should be brought up in a Christian home with appropriate teaching. Isn't that the promise that we all ask parents to make at a baptism, and why not at a wedding too? Why emphasise the division between the couple when we all want to ensure their strong, lasting marriage? We should be encouraging them both to honour their convictions and not have one override the other, for they are setting out on a life of faith and hope. I think we should regard such marriages as signs of hope."

"Thank you, Nikolas, that is very helpful. Will you write up a minute and we'll see if it could be acceptable all round. But it is a big challenge for some of us."

It looks now as a very small matter, one of those interminable petty irritations between churches, but it was a real enough issue for many young couples, torn between a church loyalty and their love for each other. It is worth recording here the proposal which came before the next meeting of the Joint Committee, first drafted by Niki and amended by other members.

"Prior to the marriage of a Catholic and a person of another Christian church, the officiating clergy will ask the couple to promise that their children, whether born to them or adopted by them, will receive Christian nurture and instruction arranged by a local congregation."

This was carried unanimously in the Committee and sent to the churches for a response. It dropped into those deep ponds. It was shuffled between the battalions. Files grew thicker. Some Vatican old-timers steamed in annoyance. The Pope's attitude was unknown but probably favoured tradition over initiative. It took eighteen months to gather all the responses, and that from the Vatican took ten pages to say, "Perhaps; we are working on it." That might be considered average progress for such discussion, for great is the difficulty that hierarchies have in facing a new idea.

Niki felt that he was getting somewhere, with growing friendships among the Geneva staff, frequent invitations to give talks and lead discussions in churches, an offer of hospitality from Princeton to do a term of study. He found that there was a welcome in Western Europe for greater understanding of the Orthodox heritage. Petrovna was enjoying her work at the child care centre and also the Geneva shopping, a stunning parade of luxury after Moscow. They had two standard holidays each year when they would return home, two weeks for the Easter celebrations and two weeks in August, when all sensible offices went to sleep.

> "I had a message from the Patriarchate this morning, saying that I was needed there over Easter for discussions, so I wonder if you would like the Moscow break or not."

> "Of course I would like to go. I always like to see how mother is managing. But there is something going on here this Easter. The Orthodox community are planning an Easter festival, with some special music and drama, and you know I have been preparing the children for their choir parts. I'd be sorry to miss that."

"Well, you have to weigh it up. But I can see that most of my time I will be confined to the offices. Not much fun for you there."

"There's another thing, Niki. I want to see a specialist to find out why I am not getting pregnant. I've thought about it a lot and I would rather try here than in Moscow; I think these doctors are more reliable. I know it's expensive but..."

"Of course it is worth a try, dear. Let's ask around for a good clinic to contact."

So just the one seat on Aeroflot was booked. As normal it was the most basic economy seat, short on leg-room. The plane was full with the passengers and their luggage, all the luxuries being taken home with pride. They landed in a cold and misty Moscow. Niki was quickly drawn into the manners and decorum of the Patriarchate, wrapped in tradition, coloured by politics, secretive by nature. It was a grand monastic compound, enclosed in high defensive walls, the church with domes gleaming in blue enamel with gold stars, a seminary for postulants, few in number, and a remarkable library with material from the thousand years of Christian history.

It had stood through the fifty years of communism because of the unwritten alliance between church and state. Always shadowed and unacknowledged, it was the church compromise with power. But it was power on both sides. The Kremlin could at any time cut off funding for the upkeep of the great historical sites, require the ending of all religious instruction and seize the church's treasures. On the other side the church had the power of devotion, the faith of millions of the older people who would be prepared to fight for the rights of the church. It may be, too, that there were senior members of the Politburo who still, beneath the veneer of Marxism, respected the mysteries of the liturgy.

Olav, the Patriarch, was very conscious of his position, dignified, slow in speech, tall, slightly stooped, with a white beard and weary blue eyes. He had carefully nurtured a relationship with President

Yumin, sending him greetings for the great saints' days and festivals, and inviting him to holiday at the old monastery at Yaroslavl where the fishing was particularly good. Yumin was not so forthcoming. He kept at the back of his mind some suspicion that the church was the breeding ground of superstition, plots and criticism. He could not express that openly, for his own position was not too secure in the bruising, bitter power struggles of the Party. His suspicion of the Orthodox was as nothing compared with his fury at the Catholics in Poland and Hungary who seemed determined to dismantle the regime.

"These church people, so confident, so wrapped in their fancy robes, how can we trust them? It was easy in the old days of the Czars, anointed by God. But here we are, with the instructions of Marx written into our minds, dealing with realities, not with visions. I'm not going to be taken in by your hospitality. I'll be polite, circumspect, and my people will keep a keen eye on anything that looks a bit unusual."

All Patriarchs, Metropolitans and Bishops were well aware of the ancient tension between state and church; it was part of their history, the air they breathed. The church had been a primary agent in the birth of the Russian state a thousand years ago. It was Russia in the presence of God, a deep belonging. Yet as the power of the Czars grew to a despotic imperium it looked like a duopoly, with the state garnering all the blessings and the church nodding approval. There was a majority cringe before communism and only sporadic church protest, quickly silenced. Retirement into the walled enclave was one solution, and that suited the state. So it was a delicate balance.

The Patriarch called Niki into his study for a discussion of his place in Geneva.

"Tell me what you understand of the benefit for your service there."

"The first thing, Father, is that it has been very helpful to have the Orthodox position represented among the top people of all the main Protestant churches. Many of them know little of us. But they are interested and there are many who actually want to learn from our theologians. I can help to inform them of our tradition and I can lead them in our prayers in the chapel there. Then I can survey the whole of the ecumenical thrust towards greater unity, the different hurdles to be overcome and the various solutions that are being translated into action in many parts of the world.

Then, perhaps the benefit that I have found most challenging and hopeful is that I am now the secretary of the Joint Vatican/WCC committee. I can see something of the Vatican attitude towards the recognition of others, the residue of its ancient claims and the little flickers of a more liberal relationship. I can be a useful channel of information."

"Thank you. I think you have done well and I am considering sustaining your service there for a further two years. I am appointing you Archdeacon. I would ask you to report to me, either in writing or in person, every six months. Now, a word of warning. Our state authorities here – and by that I mean the whole Party apparatus – are suspicious and unfriendly, not outwardly, but behind closed doors. So they may well be watching you from the embassy in Berne. Don't do anything that would give them an excuse to invade our sphere of work. No affairs with women, no political statements, no contraband when you travel – you understand me?"

"Yes, Father. I will try to be an innocent dove. But I hope more useful to you than that. Now may I have your blessing?"

***

Geneva seemed another world. On the Saturday morning after his return, Niki was sitting with Petrovna at a café table by the lake, the dramatic outflow into the river, where the full flow of snow melt water from the mountains poured like molten glass over the rock wall, mesmerising, unceasing. In the spring sunshine, with cherry and apple blossom enlivening the old gardens, it was still chilly. To Niki the city seemed to be wearing its cold face, the face of Calvin, the man who had so persuaded the sixteenth century Genevois that he had become their teacher, judge, scholar, mayor and tourist attraction. It was his cool intelligence that commanded the Reformation for much of Western Europe and his shadow which was now fading in the dubious sunrise of secularism.

"This hot chocolate is just what I needed. Now tell me about your Easter performances."

"We had a grand time. The weather was fair and there was a parade through the old town with a crowd of angels and the choir singing Easter carols. The band was supplied by the Fire Brigade. There was a great exchange of painted eggs – everyone brought some and the children were boasting of the most beautiful. Father Lukas gave a five minute talk in the square – and the loudspeakers actually worked – it was about how new life is possible even for the impossible."

"I'm so glad it worked well for you, dear. Did you go to the clinic?"

"Yes, I had the preliminary examination and the doctor said that so far they could see nothing wrong that would stop a pregnancy. But I have been having some rather odd pains in that area. They can go into it a bit deeper and they could also test you. What do you think?"

"I think we should give it a go because it's four years now without success. And this is a good place to find such expertise. I had a meeting with the Patriarch and he assured me of another two years here, so that gives us time to work things through. I don't like to think that I'm the one at fault, and you must feel the same, but we must find out. It's all a bit of a mystery."

Up at the World Council building Niki found a pile of paper on his desk. There was much talk about apartheid in South Africa and the way the churches were being drawn into the struggle. Now the Social Responsibility activists were asking the Faith and Order office for the theological response to racism. That was no simple chore, for there was plenty of racist sentiment in the Old Testament. But the task had come to Niki and he looked forward to dealing with it. The General Secretary was asking for help in approaching the Pentecostal churches in Latin America, getting onto their wavelength, to see if they would come into membership. There were questions about the wording of the Common Certificate of Baptism which most of the member churches were pledged to use. The next meeting of the Joint Catholic/WCC committee had to be arranged, agenda prepared, speakers primed. It was the turn of the Catholics to be the host, and the Secretariat in Rome had offered the hospitality of Cardinal Terracini's palatial quarters in Milan. This was promising, for it showed that the Cardinal, as head of the Secretariat for Christian Unity, regarded the work as serious, not just a social enterprise of politeness. Niki flew to Milan for a day to check out the facilities, guided by the Cardinal's household chamberlain, and found that there would be bedrooms for all the committee members in the hostel behind the church, as well as the committee room in the palace. He was told that the Cardinal would be present for one day of the three day meeting.

The committee convened in May, delightful Italian spring turning into early summer, the old lime trees around the garden of the palace in their glitter of new green. A full attendance. The Cardinal came to the opening session and gave the official welcome.

"Colleagues and friends, I am delighted to welcome you to this place which I hope will be conducive to positive work. If you are in need of anything on the domestic front, please speak to the steward who will be here at each break between sessions. Now let me assure you of the keen interest which the Holy Father takes in your work. I bring his greetings and good wishes. He asked me to say that he regards any progress towards healing ancient divisions among the followers of Christ as the work of the Holy Spirit.

We all know that issues which have divided us for a thousand years cannot be healed by a resolution of a committee, however dedicated and learned. Healing takes time. There are harsh words and bitter memories in some places. There are some fundamental differences in understanding. We all know this, my friends. But what matters is the direction in which we are travelling and you are on the right road. So I beg you, do not be put off by the weight of the task or by the slowness of our responses. Keep up the pressure.

I am sure that I don't need to remind you that we all have to carry our responsibility here on behalf of all the faithful people in our church congregations. Bring them here with you in your hearts and minds. Now, you would not expect a Cardinal to talk like that, for you probably think that I am elevated too far from local congregational life. But it is not like that for me. The more I am involved in work in the Vatican, the more I know that it is the faith of the people in the congregations, it is their struggle to believe and their hope for blessing that is crucial. That's enough from me. May the Lord bless you in these days and enjoy such hospitality as we can offer."

The members stood up and clapped politely, gathering round the Cardinal and shaking his hand. He passed a note to Niki. "Please come to my study during your lunch break. The steward will guide you."

Wondering if he had done anything to alarm or annoy the Cardinal, Niki made straight for the steward as the Committee broke at 12.30 and was led upstairs to the private quarters and a handsome study. Terracini did not appear either alarmed or annoyed but cordial.

"Now, Mr Secretary, I think that the work of the Committee is very hopeful, and you are pulling things together well, so I am grateful for that. But I want to ask you about a special piece of service which I think you could do. It is my intention – the dream of my service – to do something to begin the healing of the division between us and the Orthodox. It is now nearly a thousand years since that fateful day of formal separation and rejection. I cannot believe that it is right simply to rest on that history for another millennium. So I am planning to open a private conversation with your Patriarch. It may come to nothing, but it is right to make the effort. Now, I cannot deal with this by the normal mail, for we all know that the Kremlin may at any time have the incoming mail inspected and that your President will be opposed to any approach of any sort from Rome. But you can travel between Geneva and Moscow. I am asking you to be the link person, taking the messages in both directions. Father Jean, the Canadian member of our group in your Committee, will carry messages from Rome and pass them to you. This would be entirely confidential, a private correspondence. It is only if it shows some signs of real promise that we would share it with colleagues. Do you think you could do this service?"

Niki sat quietly for a minute, wondering if his position would be compromised by becoming such a courier.

"I think that is possible, Sir. But I have no idea at all what the Patriarch's response would be. He might object to such a way of approaching major church relationships. Or he might see it as a positive opening. You would have to wait until I can make the trip for other reasons, but I will do it and then you can tell whether it is worth continuing."

Terracini had arranged that on the second evening there would be a bus waiting for the members of the Committee to take them to the Duomo in the centre of the city for a private tour and then for their final prayers. Niki had seen the cathedral from the piazza on his previous visit, the fantasy of pinnacles, the vast bulk of it, but this was the first time he had been inside. How dark it was, the evening light hardly penetrating the gloom and the candles before the altars as faint as glow-worms. They were led around the chapels and into the crossing before the high altar where there were gleams of gold and the smell of the city pollution mixed with incense. Looking up to the ceiling, almost lost in the darkness, they saw the capitals of the great pillars were not classical forms but bundles of statuary, the human shapes lost in this dark heaven. Niki felt unbalanced, for there was something primitive here, the saints were not gilded icons met face to face, but shadows. It was an old house of an old faith, tremendous in its scale, inspiring awe for the last eight centuries, but surely not suited to the worship of the faithful, the minority of believers, amid the shopping bonanza of twentieth century Milan. Their evening prayers were muted and humbled by the space as they felt the weight of the grey stones like messages of dissent for all adventures of the spirit.

It was no surprise when, a couple of weeks later, Niki had a phone call from Father Jean to say that he had to travel to Germany for a conference and would like to drop in at Geneva on his way. He passed over a large envelope. The engagement of the courier had begun.

In his bright office, fitted with modern light furnishings, the General Secretary of the World Council of Churches, Dr Walter Schwarz, sensed trouble. He had to keep the balance between the social activists from Africa and Asia and Latin America, always eager for church pronouncements on injustice, and the churches of Europe and North America which wanted him to concentrate on matters of faith and order, unity, biblical scholarship, the ministry and ethics. It was the latter group of churches which provided almost the entire budget of the Council. So he needed to keep them in confidence. Yet the tide was turning against them. Colonialism, both political and ecclesial, was derailed, pushed into the sidings by the growth of those churches whose seeds had been sown by the missionaries.

Now it was a firm proposal by the Justice and Peace Division that the Council should have a Special Fund to Combat Racism, from which grants would be made for groups all over the world which were in the front line of the struggle. Apparently there were some wealthy liberals, perhaps with tender consciences, in America, prepared to put up the money. But the recipients of such grants might well include some way-out groups on the far left of the spectrum and some which were taking a violent path towards their objective. Could that be proper church business?

But this morning Walter Schwarz was not disturbed in his balancing act to keep all the member churches fully engaged; there was a more pressing concern. That morning he had received a letter, marked Confidential and Personal, which threatened his composure, his job and his marriage, and sent him to the toilet with a loosened bowel. It was from London. headed with the name of a firm of solicitors in Greys Inn called Williams and Gosling.

> Dear Sir,
>
> This letter refers to our client, Pamela Kissington Rona, who has requested us to write to you.
>
> She is concerned for her son, Eric, who is now needing special education because of his mental disability. She has been able to meet her costs since his birth but now finds that she cannot meet the fees for the new schooling he needs.
>
> She claims that you are the father of this child, since your sexual encounter at Oldenburg, when she was serving with the British Army and you were the rector of the seminary there.
>
> Our client is not anxious to mount a legal action, and has requested that you be approached to see whether you are prepared to give assistance.
>
> If, however, you wish to contest her claim about the paternity of her son, we would await her further instructions.
>
> Yours faithfully,
> Signed Joshua Hartington

This was lightning and thunder, a sudden punch in the guts, a storm wave against the lighthouse. Walter turned it over and over in his mind. Could it be true? Yes, it could be, he had to admit, in the dark secrecy of his memory. There was that day seven years ago, that sudden madness. She was an interpreter and administrator for the army legal service; he had visited the army base as a voluntary chaplain. They had been attracted but behaved very properly, until she had accepted his invitation to dinner, with drinks, and then went to his rooms where they fell into a long embrace and all the hasty undressing that seemed the only thing that mattered. Yes, it could be true. But Walter knew nothing of her history. Was he the only one?

What made it particularly damaging was that seven years ago Walter had been courting Lucy, who became his wife. She was the daughter of a very senior politician, brought up in a grand home in the Palatinate, was well educated, believing very strongly in the equality of women. They had met at a Lutheran church conference. Now, in Geneva, she was a striking figure of influence in the German community as well as being the senior hostess at World Council social occasions. She managed the family accounts. There was no way Walter could pay out large sums for this boy Eric without his wife's knowledge and agreement.

But if he were to contest paternity then he would have legal expenses and these would have to come from the joint account and Lucy would have to be told. Then the thought flitted through his mind, What if he could invent a social action group in England whose purpose was to fight against racism in education; then he might be able to send World Council money to a specific address. It was a fleeting thought. Of course he could not abuse the office like that. It would be bound to come out. No, better to face Lucy.

He told his personal assistant that he was not feeling well and would be at home for the day. He put the fatal letter in his brief case and made for the carpark, drove off but narrowly missed colliding with a car coming into the park, but safely reached the underground parking area under their apartment building. Going up in the lift, Walter determined to tell everything and trust that Lucy would not let anger destroy them both. He found her at the desk speaking on the phone, making arrangement for the buffet at the next meeting of the World Council Central Committee, when many senior church officers would be in Geneva. She put the phone down –

"What's happened, Walter? Are you sick?"

"I've had a big shock and could not think of anything to do but to talk with you."

"Why? What's it about?"

"I had a letter this morning and I think you had better read it, though I would like to destroy it."

He passed her the letter, sat down and waited, ready for the outburst.

"Can this be true? You look so scared that I think it must be. You stupid man! All your education and all your preaching, all those high words of faith – all were nothing when the moment came. Just as crude as a farm boy. Yes, and was it just at the time when we were going out together before the wedding? Were you crazy? The last bachelor fling – was that the idea? Was she better than your fiancée? Better legs? Better kisses?"

"No excuse, Lucy. Yes, totally, utterly stupid. The only thing I can promise is that it was a one-off and nothing like it has happened since we were married. Nothing."

"Let me think. You are in no mood to do anything useful. We must first find out how genuine this is. This woman has a solicitor so we can only reply through our lawyer. Otherwise we will put ourselves in the wrong. Call Max Thurber and see if we can see him urgently. No, I'd better do it myself."

So, at the office of Tollemarche Freres, Walter and Lucy told the sorry tale, showed the letter, and asked Max Thurber for advice, which was, for a lawyer, clear and straightforward. He was not the least dismayed; it was quite a routine business for him.

"First, we send a holding letter in reply – just that we are considering the position and will respond fully shortly. Then we engage an investigator in England to do a quick check on this woman to see if the position is as stated and what her circumstances are now. It is then only if it all adds up that we consider your responsibility. I suppose you have no address?"

"No, I've had no contact at all. The only clue that I can suggest is that I remember she spoke of her family background in Yorkshire, somewhere around Doncaster."

"Right, I'll get onto this. I know a man who can deal well with such an investigation."

Walter and Lucy faced the days ahead with churning night thoughts, silences, short conversations in carefully controlled temper and fresh assessments of each other. There was no shouting, no violent accusation. Lucy was brought up to be self-contained and competent. She had been quick to see the consequences of that letter, for it could mean the end of their Geneva appointment where she was at her best. She thought Walter was accurate in saying that he had never strayed during their marriage. So it would be best to deal with the mess as quickly as possible. But she also knew that her man was vulnerable so that in a crisis she would have to take charge. The ideal image, that early admiration, was erased – and if that was love, then she was quite prepared for their marriage to continue with a lower count on the emotional scale.

It was reassessment also for Walter. He knew that Lucy had saved him from being overwhelmed by a guilty memory; her good sense was his reinforcement. He admired her but with an edge of fear. He did not fancy a lifetime of being cushioned by her management. He was competent too, he held such a responsible job because he was efficient. But – the thought came back repeatedly – he knew that faith, habit, upbringing and the confidence of colleagues could all be lost in the moment of physical passion. That was the Achilles heel of the clergy. It made him think, not only of himself, but of all in the office, with a sharper understanding. Mercy, yes, but there's judgement too.

At the end of a week, Max Thurber asked them to call and hear the report.

"The investigator found it easy to trace Pamela Rona from the army records. She had returned to UK and the Catterick base, and from there was demobilised. Her address was then given as Croydon, in South London. And there my man, John Rogers, picked her up in the marriage records. She was married to Richard Brian Scopes at the Registry Office on October 10th, 1960."

"That was just two months after I was with her that August."

"Yes, well, Scopes was also in the army. He was a captain in the tank regiment stationed near Oldenburg and was still serving when they married. But then two further records came to light. The first was the birth notice for their baby, Eric, born on March 6th 1961. The second was the death certificate of Captain Scopes, who died in a road accident on the A22 on 20 January 1962 during a heavy fog. I think that this is a pretty good result from a week's work. It gives us the picture of this woman making a hasty marriage, probably because she knew she was pregnant, but then losing her husband and being left with the child."

"But it could be that she was having an affair with Scopes in Germany and that it was his baby."

"Yes, Mrs Schwarz, that is so. Since Scopes is dead there will be only Pamela's word on whether they had a sexual connection at that time."

"Did your man actually see Pamela and Eric?"

"Yes, from the electoral register he found that she was resident in Selsdon, near Croydon, so he was able to see that it was a house divided into flats, rather run down property, and he saw them walking, presumably to the school, one morning. He only saw them from the back but they seemed to walk normally and were dressed in rather poor clothes, not at all smart. He took this picture – not very clear."

Lucy and Walter gazed at the picture. Could this be Walter's son? Who could possibly tell? At least they now knew that the original letter had not been entire fiction; there was a child. There might be a case for them needing help. What was the next step?

"It seems to me that you have to select one of the two options. You could take the line that you agree to send some financial support. Or you could dispute the paternity on account of Pamela Rona's relationship with Captain Scopes. The former option would suggest that you accept paternity and that would open you to repeated claims over the years. So I would advise the second."

So it was agreed that the lawyers would correspond. The paternity issue had to be settled before there could be any consideration of financial support. It meant a period of uncertainty, not easy for a religious leader with a tender conscience, so Walter needed a full recovery of his old life with Lucy, the old tenderness and confidence.

He could not live at an arms-length formality with his wife; that would be the mere shell of a marriage. Yet neither of them found it easy to speak the words of love. The heart may be yearning, reaching out, longing to embrace but the reticence of the years trapped them both.

Two things came together to bring release. The first was when Walter attended the staff mid-day prayers in the lovely light chapel, the best part of the Council building, with a Korean leading. The lectionary reading was about the betrayal of Jesus by Peter and the dramatic cockcrow which revealed his failure. Dr Kim Guo spoke of the gift of self-knowledge as the way to redemption, "we are often brought to reality by a cockcrow of events, reminding us of what we are, such fallible disciples. But that is the path of reality; that is where the Lord meets us so that we can make a new beginning." Yes, thought Walter, that is surely the basis for our marriage, the reality of what we are. I must share that with Lucy. Then came the opportunity, which was Lucy's birthday. After the very conventional presents – a silk scarf, a silver-backed hair brush and a potted dwarf hydrangea – Walter held her close.

"I need you, dear, because we both know that I was very foolish, and we don't yet know that the outcome will be; but you are the partner of my life and I love you and admire you; I don't want you just as the strong colleague; I want you close, open in every way as I would be for you."

And he embraced her with such eagerness that it could have bruised her, yet bruises of love were not to be despised. She knew that if the marriage was to work, then Walter must be allowed to be strong and efficient and wise, allowed, encouraged and loved. She kissed him, the kiss of Yes we are always together. They were interrupted by the phone, a call from their daughter Rachel, who was just starting work as a librarian in Hamburg, to give her mother a happy birthday greeting. The sun was shining in the clear air of early summer, the swallows were nesting under the broad eaves and it was like a new year's day of grace for them both. For a moment they could forget the grey cloud in the north.

As part of the preparation for the Central Committee meeting, Niki flew to Moscow for two days to consult with the Patriarch about the agenda and anything that the Orthodox might wish to put forward for discussion. So that was the occasion to hand over the letter from Cardinal Terracini.

> Your Grace, we send you our fraternal greetings from the Secretariat for Christian Unity in the Vatican. We know you as brothers in the faith of our Lord, we admire your steadfastness and we pray that you may be blessed in all your service.
>
> I am writing to you in a very personal and confidential way. I do this because I am not sure of the way forward. But my motive is plain. It is part of my duty and calling in this position to seek fresh ways of bringing greater unity to the people of God. You will realise what a difficult task that is, but a task given to us by our Lord who prayed for the unity of his followers.
>
> So, as an important part of that calling, I seek to find ways in which the ancient division between Rome and the Orthodox might be bridged. Of course that is a long-term

hope. There is no way in which a thousand years of separation can be overcome in short negotiations. But sometime, somewhere we have to make a start.

My suggestion is that you and I correspond about the barriers which have to be overcome, to see whether there are any ways through which would be possible for us both. This would be an entirely private correspondence, for if it reveals to us no hope at all then it would be foolish to have encouraged the councils of the two communions. But if, after a year or two, we do see some points of light, then we might agree to share with our colleagues.

I know that such a suggestion may come to you as something risky, since we all understand that the Kremlin would not welcome any rapprochement with Rome. So it is up to you to decide whether my suggestion is a positive one. I have asked Nicholas Demenchov, who is a very helpful presence in Geneva, to carry these letters, and I trust that is agreeable to you.

Your fellow-servant in Christ,
Terracini

It was read with astonishment by Olav and with understanding by Niki. Could it possibly be true that the Vatican was actively seeking some way through towards friendship, even towards reconciliation? Could the Cardinal have written like that without the knowledge of the Pope? And why Moscow? What of Athens and Istanbul? But what an opening! If he could be the one to take this opportunity seriously, and if there were some signs of progress, then it would be the most significant work of the Patriarchate for centuries. It would be historic.

"You have met Terracini, Nicholas. What do you think of his intentions and his character?"

"Sir, I was as surprised as you are when he spoke to me in Milan. But I think we have to take him seriously, for he is a scholarly man, not given to sudden enthusiasms, and his presidency of the Secretariat is his major present duty at the Vatican. He stresses that this is a private conversation, but I do not think he could have written that letter without some hint from the Pope. So I do not see that we could lose anything by replying in a positive way. It is all very exploratory. You could call it off at any time if you were to see no points of light at all. But I agree that we would have to keep it quiet, especially from the Kremlin."

"Yes, and then, if we were to decide to go public it would have to be with such widespread publicity and such a big occasion that even the Party could not trample on us."

Niki carried the positive reply back to Geneva, where it was collected by Father Jean. Niki had been thinking during the flight of the points at which the two communions were divided. There were the lesser disagreements and then the very major hurdle. The wording of the creed, the church calendar, the marriage of priests, the pattern of the liturgy, and even trivial things like beards – all would have to be put on the table before the really major issue, the authority of the Bishop of Rome as the human head of the church universal and the more recent issue of papal infallibility. It was daunting, a Himalaya to cross. The secular world would see it all as petty church politics, but those involved in church life and all who knew some church history would realise that here was a genuine attempt to overcome a millennium of separation.

Then in July the meeting of the World Council Central Committee was convened, with 200 representatives from member churches gathered in the main hall at the Geneva building. There were senior figures, archbishops, moderators, theologians among them, and also a sprinkling of local pastors, women and younger people. There were young people acting as stewards, passing out the multiple sheets of discussion papers and providing headphones, for the interpreters in their cubicles were translating into English, French, Spanish and Russian. On the platform were the seven Presidents, chosen for a spread of the continents and the faith traditions, and the General Secretary, who was called on to make the opening address.

Walter had pushed aside his personal worries as he prepared that text. He took as his theme the well-known verse in Matthew chapter 6, "Set your mind on God's kingdom and his justice before everything else, and all the rest will come to you as well." He described how this applied to all the departments of the Council's work, to the support for refugees, to evangelism, to environmental concerns and ethical dilemmas, to the struggle against racism and to the being of the church itself. The talk was well received, but soon forgotten. Discussion then began on the departmental reports and the budget. The most difficult debate was on the Programme to Combat Racism and the grants which were listed as having been made to the African National Congress in South Africa, which was known to be actively preparing military schemes of disruption. The word used by a Scottish Moderator was "grants to terrorists." This set the African members leaping to their feet and hugging the microphone. "A century of pleading, suffering, pleading, abuse, a century of oppression – then how do we go on pleading in calm voices – how is it wrong to stir things up – their violence against us is permissible in your eyes – how can you, from the comfort of your sleepy Scottish parish, tell us we are wrong?"

As General Secretary, Walter asked to speak. "Let us be clear that the aim is racial justice. That is true to the text from which we started this morning. We are faced with the situation of a minority oppressing a majority on the basis of race, a minority with the political and military power of the state. This has to be opposed by all who seek justice. The programme of this Council is to provide assistance for the educational and humanitarian work of the ANC, to provide legal aid and support for the families of those in gaol. We cannot, from Geneva, control the expenditure of the grants but we are assured by the South African Council of Churches that the leadership of the ANC is responsible and will use the grants wisely and not for military purposes. Let us trust them. I ask the members of the Committee to approve the work of this Programme of the Council because it is a key moment in the history of justice for Africa."

When the vote was taken those opposing were few, the more conservative Lutherans and some Scots and Irish Presbyterians, and two from the southern states of the US, perhaps twenty in all, and all of them white. The dissent would rumble on. In the next months Walter was showered with angry letters from individuals and congregations opposing the grants, many from Baptists and Presbyterians. So it was ironical that on the last evening of the gathering the members were taken by bus to the old city for a service of worship and praise in the ancient auditorium of Jean Calvin, now used as a Presbyterian church. As they sung metrical psalms many thoughts wandered. There the old reformer had preached his way in countless sermons through all the chapters of the New Testament. There his clarity in writing and speaking had been persuasive. There the chalice was first shared with the laity. There the hazy glory of the medieval church was dispelled. Yet it was a cold light, that of Calvin. In all the thousand pages of his great work, the Institutes of the Christian Religion, we do not hear the cry of a child in the night.

So the members left Geneva, to meet again in eighteen months, at New Delhi, invited by the member churches in India and the East Asia Christian Conference. That would be a very different experience from sanitised Switzerland. Walter wondered if he would still be the person to organise that agenda.

The question was soon settled. Max Thurber asked Walter and Lucy to call at his office. "You will know that the specimen you provided, Walter, and that provided by Eric, were sent to the laboratory in Oxford. They have sent their report to me and to Williams and Gosling in London. The report is clear and decisive. They state that there is no possibility that you are the father of Eric. That will be a great relief to you both. It naturally suggests to us that Captain Scopes was the father, but we have no need to establish that. Now, what do you wish me to do? Do you wish simply to close the correspondence since we have no responsibility? Or do you have any other considerations?"

"There's nothing more to be done," Walter was sure, as he rode the wave of relief.

"Anything we might do, like providing some financial help to Pamela, would be an opening for constant appeals, so we would become involved, when there is no reason for it."

"I agree," said Max, "and I wonder whether there is not some army widow's pension which Pamela can claim and some special assistance for her autistic son. The UK social security network is usually comprehensive. I will write to Williams and Gosling to end the correspondence, saying that there is no purpose in pursuing a matter which is now closed on the evidence provided."

They drove back to their apartment as though sailing on a cloud and opened a bottle of wine for lunch. Walter knew that it was a lucky escape; he could easily have been the one. Good resolutions floated across the lunch table. There was no such easy resolution for Niki and Petrovna.

The doctor at the specialist clinic had advised Petrovna to have some X-rays done; these revealed that there was a shadow of some sort of growth which would have to be investigated. "Not a big problem, but one which must be cleared up," he said. This meant an operation in hospital, a very expensive exercise. Niki spoke by phone to Moscow to ask if there would be cover by the church for this expense. Yes, the answer was prompt, for we know that the standards in Geneva will ensure the best outcome.

The operation proved to be serious, the removal of an ovarian cyst and a hysterectomy, leaving Petrovna weak, facing a long period of careful recuperation. Niki met the surgeon and asked for her assessment. "We are confident that we have cleared all the growth. But the analysis shows us that the cyst was malignant. So that means we shall have to watch carefully for the next two or three years. I am not suggesting any further treatment just now, but six monthly checks will be essential. The key at the moment is rest and no worry, so I suggest that you do not tell your wife that the cyst was malign; just keep that in your mind."

Niki knew that he could not nurse Petrovna properly and still keep his work schedule, at least not for long. He phoned her mother in Moscow to give the news and ask whether Petrovna could stay with her for a month or two. She was immediately welcoming and saw it as a great opportunity to bring some fresh meaning to her dull life. After a fortnight the doctor said that they could fly to Moscow provided there were special provisions for comfort at the two airports and on the plane. All the authorities played their parts well, even the utilitarian Aeroflot found that a special seat at the front of the plane that usually was kept for a top politician, would on this date be available. So on the second week of August they arrived in Moscow and Petrovna had a great, embracing welcome from her mother, who had garnered all the fresh fruit and vegetables and had done all the cooking, to treat her daughter with what luxury she could possibly afford.

Niki delivered the latest Terracini letter to the Patriarch.

> Your Grace, I am indebted to you for such a gracious response. We may be tempted to speed towards great visions and resolutions, but I will try to be as practical as possible as we discuss these ancient barriers. If you find that I am going too fast, please tell me frankly.
>
> I would like to begin with two areas of disagreement which I believe can be faced with realism and hope.
>
> The first is the 'filioque' clause in the creed. Here I sense that there is some willingness on the part of the Vatican to move – not by any means a decision, but at least a readiness for discussion. The credal formula that the Spirit "proceedeth from the Father and the Son" has a complex history. We trace "and the Son" back to the Council of Toledo in 447 after which it was taken up and used widely in the Western church. In 867 Pope Nicholas 1 was excommunicated by Photius, Bishop of Constantinople for having corrupted the creed by this addition. It remained in the Western version but was never used in the East.
>
> It has often been supported on the basis of John 15:26 and John 16:7 where Jesus told his disciples that "I will send him (the Spirit) to you." In the light of modern biblical scholarship I do not see those references as determinative. Those chapters in John, 14 to 17, can hardly be read as

verbatim sayings of Jesus, for passages of such length were not recorded on the spot, but rather should be read as meditations on his words which were their core.

But the strongest reason for leaving dogmatism behind is that we cannot humanly define the interior life of the Triune God. We are dealing with mystery. We have no human images or words that are adequate to the task. Our part is to be thankful for the life of the Spirit, believing that this is God active in relation to the world.

I am therefore ready to press towards dropping the "filioque" from the creed so that we all speak with one voice. I believe this might lead to agreement.

On the second issue I am suggesting that we move in the other direction, that is, for the Gregorian calendar to be accepted by the Orthodox. All calendars are human inventions and are not set down for us in the Bible or in the early rulings of the Fathers. The Gregorian calendar has proved to be acceptable throughout the world and for all practical purposes is universal. Would it not be possible for you to look at this as a matter of practicality rather than of faith? We would then be able to celebrate Easter at one time as one family of God.

Thank you for giving your time and thought to these matters. I hope you can see them as opportunities for progress.

Grace and Peace Terracini

Patriarch Olav and Niki worked together on the response. Greatly pleased by the first point at issue, Olav was more doubtful over the second, knowing how deeply the Russian people were persuaded that their dating for Easter was correct. He was very ready to accept that for all practical purposes the Gregorian calendar had to be used, so the Western church Easter would always be a sacred day and there was no reason why the Eastern church should not worship in sympathy. But the Eastern Easter would never be neglected. Olav thought that one possibility might be to declare that it was a special festival day for Mary Magdalene, the witness in the garden at dawn. It could also become the celebration of the service of women, and that would have wide appeal. But to get any sort of approval for this from all the Orthodox churches would be a major test, not something that could be rushed. He ended his letter suggesting that the next topic might be the marriage of priests – for that would be a great hurdle for the Vatican.

Niki travelled with the letter and settled down to take up the pile of work on his desk. During the summer the Faith and Order Division had been joined by a young English woman, Elspeth Beach, who had been recommended by the Archbishop of York. She was his niece. She had graduated in language studies and was also an efficient office organiser, so the staff welcomed her with open arms. She was able to do some of the translation work when the official translators were hard pressed with long papers on 'Caring for Bangladesh Flood victims', 'The United Church of Canada's struggle over Homosexual Pastors', 'Justice for Amerindians', and 'The ethics of abortion in rape cases', and many others, all no doubt worthy efforts but demanding much time for translation. Elspeth Beach proved her ability to shortcut the process. The Director of Faith and Order was Dr Miriam Menzies from the Church of Scotland, who had been a university lecturer in theology at St Andrews. Niki was her deputy. He became uncomfortably aware that Elspeth Beach was attracted to him.

In fact she was deeply drawn, magnetised. She loved his voice, his style, his quick understanding and his manners. She admired the touch of mystery that always came from a Russian background and the fortitude of the church under communism. She took care to sit beside Niki in departmental meetings, and looked for him at the lunch counters. Any work she did for him always seemed to need frequent discussion. Niki was not armoured against admiration but had learned that for the clergy a fan club, a common misdirection of emotion, must always be held at arm's length. He became alarmed when, on a wet afternoon in October, he felt bound to offer Elspeth a lift in his car after work. She had accepted so eagerly, looked at him with such delight, that he wondered if he had been foolish. But it was too late to retract.

When they reached her apartment block, she pressed towards him and asked him to come in for a hot drink. On the spot, his thoughts tumbled. Yes, and what might follow. Yes, and she did look very willing. No, he could not bring shame to Petrovna. No, the Patriarch had warned him. But yes, he was just a man. How much can pass through the mind in a second and through the body too. That day caution won, for the word came back to him, Never ever have an affair in the office. Emotionally shaken, Niki made it home and, in his relief tried to phone Petrovna in Moscow, but the connection was only possible with long delay. He determined to have a talk with Dr Miriam next morning.

"Miriam, I need to share with you a very personal thing and ask your advice. It is about Elspeth. I am aware that she has been dealing with a lot of my work and that she comes to my room very often and seems to be attracted to me. I don't want to hurt her. But I can't encourage her either. I wonder if you have noticed this."

"Yes, Nicholas, I have certainly noted it. It's pretty obvious. But she is such a good worker and valuable that I don't want to move her from Faith and Order. We have never had such an able assistant."

"But we are only a small unit, so I can't possibly avoid her."

"I understand that, and I guess the fact that Petrovna is in Moscow might make things particularly difficult."

"Yes, I feel that and I know that I must not get entangled."

"How would it be if I make Elspeth my personal assistant so that she has more of my work to do and less of yours. I would get to know her better and it might get to the point when she confides in me and we can talk freely. For your part, perhaps you could be just a bit more formal. I doubt if this will solve the problem, but it might make for a way of working that doesn't end in tears."

"That's a great help, Miriam. And perhaps she will meet others and find a new attachment. Isn't love such a heartache, so hard to navigate. Is this a relic of our animal origin which we still have not got under control, a primal urge?"

"Well, it is surely part of our physical nature but we have brought to it such hopes and desires and conventions that it has become a feature of our humanity, this longing for intimate connection which goes far beyond mere animal attraction. Yes, and far beyond the financial arrangements between families."

"Do you think Augustine was right to see the devil at work in sex?"

"No, Nicholas, I have long ceased to think in such terms. What is instinctive in us is not evil, it is just primitive. The physical desire for sex and the physical desire for food are both natural hungers and we cannot call them evil. But we have to keep some sort of control for the sake of peace and to avoid hurting other people. Those old letters of St Paul were strong on the control, but he did not seem to appreciate the joy of intimacy; that seems to me a gap in Paul's teaching and so Augustine, who was following Paul, rather went overboard on the subject. And that has been one-sided thinking in the church ever since."

"It is so good to talk, Miriam, and thanks."

"I'm just hoping we can hold things together. We all learn that there are some problems that have to be lived with, for there is no immediate solution. I am old enough to be a sort of aunt for Elspeth. We need not tell her uncle, the Archbishop, about that."

4

It was a cold November when Niki flew to Moscow to bring Petrovna back to Geneva. She had recovered well, had put on some weight but was now tired of the little Moscow flat and the very limited supply of fresh fruit and vegetables. Her mother queued and cooked and enjoyed having her daughter at home, but it had been long enough. Beetroot and cabbage deserve a star for 'boring.'

Niki also carried the latest Terracini letter, coming to one of the toughest questions that lay between the two traditions, that of married clergy.

> "You, my dear Patriarch, have put this topic on the table, and rightly so, for it is deeply entrenched in our communions. The best thing I can do is to express the foundations of our thinking on the matter, so that you can see what a major task we have ahead.
>
> Priestly celibacy became the way for us through the monastic movement. From the time of St Benedict it was the religious communities which stood firm during the upheavals of the Middle Ages. They were the lasting witnesses to the Gospel. They preserved the text itself. It was their ministry which kept the church alive. So the parish priest was like an extension of the monastery,

offering the same personal commitment. Celibacy was a vital part of that tradition, and has been ever since. So it is a long story.

It has proved itself in our history. Celibacy set the priesthood free from family responsibility so that every priest could be totally committed and devoted to the service of the church. He did not have to worry about his wife wanting a new kitchen or his daughter keeping the household awake when she was teething. He was not trapped into family or clan disputes. Also he was able to respond if his bishop needed him to serve in another place – no problems in moving. This has been and still is a very great help in the evangelisation of remoter places. You can't imagine Matthew Ricci or Francis Xavier travelling as they did with a family to care for.

We would not wish to dilute this total commitment. Surely there must be many situations where a married priest has a divided loyalty – to the family and to the parish. Do you not find that this is a difficulty?

We would also be concerned that there are such things as failed marriages, there are domestic disputes, there are betrayals. This is a reality for the world and married priests cannot be isolated or hidden if the worst happens – then it is public shame for the church. How do you cope with that?

Then at a lower level of concern, the support for a married priest is surely expensive, and there are many parts of the world where the church could not find the resources to house and care for a family. We could not readily accept this extra burden.

So there is a lot to consider, and all we can do, in this correspondence is to see whether there are any likely points of negotiation. I am very ready to hear your response."

"What a good correspondent Terracini is." Olav smiled with appreciation. "This deserves a very careful answer because he is being very clear that this is of primary importance."

It took them some time. Niki found that although Olav was learned in the history and the theology, he was not very adept in forming a cohesive argument. So it was a matter of taking down pages of notes and then shaping them into a reasonable letter.

"I am very grateful to you for setting out your position regarding married priests, and here I try to respond. Please let me know if I am not clear or if I am missing important matters.

As you know, the Orthodox tradition is that celibacy is optional for priests, it is a personal choice. Our monastic tradition is at one with you, celibacy is part of the vows. That has stood the test of time, although numbers in religious communities have been falling for a generation. But for parish priests marriage is also an option. This matter of choice seems to us be in tune with the human character – what is right for some is not right for others. God does not call all to the same way of life.

Does it work? Is there the same commitment? It is a good question. But think of it this way. Is a married brain surgeon less committed to his profession than a celibate? Does a married police inspector strive less to catch criminals because he has a family? We would all surely reply No. We do not find a dilution of commitment. The married priest is available to his people, performs the same duties, seeks the same goals, bears the same burdens as a celibate priest.

But more than that, there is a plain advantage that a married priest can enter fully into the normal problems of family life, he knows it from the inside, he understands what it means to sacrifice for the sake of the children, he knows what sexual delight may be, he knows something of the tough family budget. He is at one with the majority. That makes it much more likely that people will open their lives and their hearts to him.

A further benefit is that the wife of the priest may be ready to discuss matters with women which a man would never hear. She may, in many rural areas, be able to help with a clinic or an infant school. The home may become a shelter for women suffering domestic violence. All that depends on personalities and circumstances, but is often a blessing.

You are right in thinking that a married priest is not so mobile, but as we also have celibate priests that is not a particular problem.

The cost is also something that has to be thought about and I can see that any sudden increase in costs would be a big problem for the Catholic Church. We expect that any parish with a married priest will provide the basic stipend and will also help with produce if available. The diocese has to keep an eye on this to ensure that no one is in hardship and there are times when the local funds have to be supplemented.

Then you raise the question about marriages that fail and cause shame or sorrow for the church. It is true. This is one of the cares of every bishop. But I ask you to think for a minute about the problems of celibate clergy. Don't you have to deal with men who get into trouble with women? Surely that has been a scandal through the centuries. And what of men who are homosexual by nature, aren't they a problem for you? Or men who lose their faith and convictions? I am just trying to say that since we are all dealing with the humanity we share, there will always be some people who in some way fail to honour their ordination vows, but I do not think that is any more common a problem for the married than the unmarried.

A quite basic matter for us – and for you – is that there is no command from Our Lord about celibacy, and indeed no objection to married apostles, with Peter as a model. So any ruling that we may make is a human prescription, to be judged for its wisdom and its charity.

Perhaps I have written enough for this point in our conversation. Let us keep along this track of exploration."

***

The cold weather came early to Geneva that year. The mountains were white against a grey sky and the great lake was an uninviting smoky green. Two days of wet weather had frozen on the cobbled streets of the old town. Taxi drivers were impatient and windows were fogged. Lights came on mid-afternoon. Niki was anxious to get home from a seminar at a church in the Rue de Choiseul and was on the pavement when two men approached him, one from each side. They were big and looked tough. Niki immediately thought they were trouble and turned to run up the hill behind him. The man on his left made a lunge for him, slipped on a patch of ice and crashed down on the pavement, dislocating his shoulder, shouting in anger and pain. The other man's attention was distracted for a moment and Niki was able to run. He ran upwards and then turned into a narrow alley, saw a well-lit café and rushed inside. Out of breath, he found a seat at a small table and ordered tea with lemon, watching the door and the shadows of those outside.

He realised that he could have trapped himself and could not sit over a cup of tea for an hour. He asked if he could use the phone at the back of the café and called the police, explaining who he was and asking for assistance. The police on the desk questioned the need.

"I ran to evade these two thugs who were coming for me and who looked dangerous."

"But why did you think there was some danger?"

"Because, when one slipped and hurt himself on an icy patch, he swore and swore in Russian."

"How did they arrive?"

"Not sure, but it looked as though they had come in a Volkswagon Beetle which was stopped by the curb."

"I'll get a man to that café and he will escort you here to the station to make a statement."

Confused and worried, Niki did his best to tell the story. He was sure that the men were Russian, but whether thugs bent on robbery or KGB operators – but, of course, Russians picking on him as a Russian, that could not be just accidental, it must be organised, must be political. He was driven home by the police and told to be careful.

"We will try to trace the car. What colour was it?"

"It was under the street light and looked white but might have been another light colour."

"We will soon see whether there is anything like that registered to a Russian owner."

As Petrovna and Niki talked, he became clearer in his mind that this must be an incident related to his connection with Father Jean and the Cardinal and the letters, for there was nothing else that marked him out from all the other staff of the World Council. If, somehow, the Kremlin had become suspicious, then the whole thing would become inoperable and there might be further dangers. He determined that he would tell the whole story to Miriam Menzies and to Walter Schwartz, for the work was of such importance they must find a way ahead.

"This is personal and confidential but it is also about our work," Niki explained to them in Walter's office next day. "I have to tell you a story that I have not shared because it was given to me in confidence. It started with the Joint Committee with the Vatican Secretariat. Cardinal Terracini asked me to become the courier for correspondence with my Patriarch in Moscow about a possible way towards reconciliation between Rome and the Orthodox. It was very private because they did not want to raise any expectations if the letters showed no prospects whatever of movement to reconciliation. I carried the letters in both directions to avoid any chance that the Kremlin would get hold of them and then punish the church for having dealings with Rome, just now that the Catholic Church has become so vigorous in Hungary and Poland against their regime.

But yesterday I was caught in town by a couple of thugs who spoke Russian. I was able to get away and call the police. I have no idea who they were or what they intended to do. But I can only think that they were in some way connected with the Russian network. Perhaps the embassy in Bern has become suspicious of my travels to and from Moscow. You see, I feel that Petrovna and I may be some kind of target. And this piece of work may be at risk, just when it was beginning to grapple with the big issues between East and West. So I have told you what I know and ask for your suggestions and wisdom."

"This is extraordinary," Miriam could hardly believe the account, "for two such high ranking people to open a correspondence. It suggests to me that the Pope must have authorised it. But I can see that it puts the Patriarchate at some risk. What a wonderful thing it would be if this could actually lead towards a reconciliation."

"Yes," said Walter, "it is a very important matter and we must not jeopardise it. But there is another aspect to this which strikes me because of the office I hold. If this becomes public then there could be difficulties with the Protestant churches – members of the Council – who might see themselves squeezed out of the discussion, and this mighty block pushing them into the background."

"Yes, I understand that," Niki said, "and that is a strategic matter we must think about. But today what do you suggest for my own part in it all?"

"I've an idea," Miriam was quick to see possibilities. "How would it be if we ask Niki and Petrovna to move out to Bossey to join the staff there? It is a secluded property. It is easy to be aware of comings and goings. Niki could do much of his work there. We could arrange that the daily delivery takes his work to and fro. Petrovna might take over the care of the Blue Angels, for they need a bit of supervision."

"But how can we continue to help the correspondence? Surely it is a fitting ecumenical task."

"How would it be if I, as General Secretary, ask my German embassy in Bern if we could put letters to the Patriarch in the diplomatic bag? I don't think the Russian authorities would dare to mess with that."

"That's a brilliant suggestion. But I will have to phone the Cardinal and the Patriarch to see if it all clear with them."

"But why," asled Miriam, "if we are dealing with diplomatic channels, does not the Cardinal deal direct using the Vatican or the Italian diplomatic bag?"

"I think I know the answer that might come from the Cardinal to that suggestion. The Patriarch likes me to help with the correspondence. He is excellent at seeing the main points, but likes some help in framing the replies. He thinks I can put things in an appealing way. Then the other reason is that the Cardinal knows how strongly the Kremlin distrusts Rome. The situation in Eastern Europe makes the Russians suspicious of anything coming from Rome, and it is not impossible that they would hold and open the bag. I don't know about that but I think that is in the Cardinal's mind."

"Let's think it over for a day or so. As General Secretary I will accept responsibility for any decisions here. Nicholas, will you talk it over with Petrovna tonight and let me know tomorrow if you agree to the Bossey idea. Then Miriam, it would be up to you to arrange the work plan. You might think of the Joint Committee meeting at Bossey."

That evening Niki and Petrovna settled the matter. They were at ease with each other. Petrovna was a neat, compact, attractive woman. With short blonde hair and with her wide smile, she might have been a model for one of the Soviet posters of the happy worker. She was still deeply in love, still longing for a child, but was a realist knowing that pregnancy was not for her. She was content to agree with the Bossey suggestion, and once settled there they would think about adoption.

In fact the move was a good prospect. The old chateau had been given to the World Council of Churches in the days after WW2 as a place where pastors and their wives from the ruined cities of Europe might have respite and peace and good food for a holiday. From that it developed to become the Ecumenical Institute, a study centre. Students came to do a graduate course from October to May and in the summer short courses were offered for groups such as Bible translators or church administrators or musicians or a dozen other specialisations. To care for the house and its domestic life, girls from the European churches came as staff, known as Blue Angels from their uniform. The whole property, with chapel and garden, was 15 kilometres from the city along the north coast of the lake. In summer, with the long grass in the paddock, geraniums flattering the old stone and the lake shimmering below, it was a desirable place to be.

***

After a meeting of the Central Committee of the Communist Party, President Yumin called two of the members, reliable old cronies, into his office, settled them in easy chairs, poured the vodka and opened the discussion.

"I've been wondering a lot recently about the church. Why is it still here? Why hasn't it faded away? Isn't it just a relic of the old thinking? We pay our dues in order to calm the public nerves, but isn't it all a façade?"

"Yes, and all the churches are the same, all built on such shaky foundations – you know, ancient quarrels, kings against bishops. It's as though the fairy stories of childhood have been built up into a solemn adult textbook."

"But, President, there must be more to it than that. Do people die for the sake of a fairy story? I had an uncle Gregor who walked in bare feet every day for three months to reach Kiev for a saint's day and nearly died in the cold. There's a very strong appeal there."

"Well, I can't believe in God. God does nothing. Pray for a good harvest and it's washed away in the rain. Pray for your wife with cancer and she dies. It must be a dream. Surely everyone can see that."

"I think it's what they call "wishful thinking" in the West. People would like it to be true that there is some kind and powerful ruler of history."

"We've been the rulers here and I've never heard a God-voice telling me what to do."

"The priests say that God talks in the church through the holy book and the saints, but if you ask them to prove it, they can't."

"And if we take a thousand priests and silence them in the camps, the people will call them saints and call us devils. So I guess we just have to live with them. It's a mystery to me."

"I think, President, you have said the right word. It is a mystery. It's not Marxist or rational thinking. It's unproven. God is never showing himself. But there's some corner of the mind that senses a mystery, and the church says, Come and let us approach it together. It's a little window, so look here for the glory. So they dress the church with gold and light the candles before the icons and the priest bows to the chalice and the old chant echoes around the dome, all to say that here you are carried towards the mystery. It's a drama."

"I can accept that. But, by all the gods, I'll keep a close watch on their ambitions and schemes. Now I'm going to bed."

5

It was late in the evening in the Patriarch's private quarters when his valet heard shouting from the bathroom. He ran in, sure it was his boss in trouble. He opened the bathroom door and saw Olav on the floor, doubled up in pain, vomiting, shivering, white faced. He called out and then remembered the panic button which was in the bedroom, switched it on, went back to hold Olav's head up from the floor, wiped his mouth, pulled him into a sitting position with his back to the wall. The private secretary came running, saw the crisis and phoned for an ambulance.

The old man was unconscious when they reached the hospital. The doctors soon diagnosed that there was food poisoning of some sort. "What had he been eating?"

"He did not eat very much," said the valet, "Just a small piece of salmon with new potatoes at dinner and then, when he went to bed at 10.30 he had a bread roll with butter and a glass of milk."

A sample of the vomit was sent to the lab with orders for a quick analysis. The police were informed, arrived at speed and looked around the Patriarch's rooms, taking with them the remains of the bread roll and the tumbler.

"Who had access to the preparation of his food?"

"The cook in the main kitchen prepared the dinner and I dealt with the late night snack in the kitchenette off the dressing room."

"Who else could get in?"

"Any of the staff here could have entered the kitchen. No-one else could have been in these rooms."

The police inspector thought that it could easily have been some contamination in the salmon, perhaps only lightly cooked, perhaps not as fresh as it should have been. The hospital report was plain. There was poison in the stomach, not from the salmon or the milk but somehow mixed into the little new potatoes, as though it had been injected with a hypodermic needle. The report was immediately seized by the police.

The report in Pravda next day had a brief account. The Patriarch was in intensive care in hospital after food poisoning. He was expected to recover. The police had discovered that the problem was the fish supplied for dinner; it was not fresh and had not been properly frozen. The fish supplier was being sought.

"I suppose," muttered Alexei, the Dean of the seminary, as he read the paper, "they will discover that the fish wholesaler was a Chechen."

But, in the Russian fashion, the case went dead. Olav slowly recovered, but it soon became clear that he was not able to carry the old load of work. He asked for Niki to come for a visit, for he needed to make sure that the correspondence that had begun with Rome could continue. It was too important to lapse. When the German embassy phoned to say that they had a package for the Patriarch, he sent two reliable men from the seminary and they had brought it back safely. How odd, he thought, that a conversation about theology should become a matter for secret couriers. Perhaps it was time to go public.

The cardinal wrote with understanding for the new conditions of the correspondence, but worried for the risks involved. He went on to the main topic of married priests.

"Your letter was very helpful and persuasive. I am reassured by your wide experience. I do not know whether my colleagues here would be ready to engage with such a radical change, but personally I would regard the option as possible.

But there is another factor that puzzles me. Your tradition makes it clear that although a parish priest may be married, a bishop may not be. He is always from among the celibate clergy. How did this distinction arise? Is it to do with monasticism? We should not propose a radical change in our tradition that would still leave us in the position that the celibate state is somehow more holy and responsible than marriage; that would be a false distinction from which we have tended to suffer too long. I look forward to your thoughts on this.

I am persuaded that we have found enough hope in this correspondence to approach the great issue between our communions, that of papal authority. Despite all the lesser issues, I know that it has been the great rock on which the unity of the church has been wrecked. There has always been great passion on both sides. I stand within the tradition that the Bishop of Rome has the authority to speak and to act for the whole body of the world church, he is the focal point of unity. You know the Gospel passages on which this conviction was based, the declaration of Christ regarding St Peter.

I must confess that I do not see any possibility of walking away from that central belief and practice. But sometimes, when I am praying and studying, I think of our hopes and I dare to imagine ways forward.

There is an old saying that there are more ways of killing a cat than drowning it in cream. So there are more ways of moving a tradition that denying it. Take, for example, the doctrine of papal infallibility as it was propounded in 1870 at Vatican 1. At that time it was largely a response to political insecurity and the need to bolster papal authority. They took up an unwritten tradition and turned into a doctrine of the church. It is now not possible for the church simply to cancel what was written then. But it is possible to ignore it, to let it lapse, to watch it fade into the past, unused. And that is happening.

So I can imagine that, in a more inclusive synod or council, the Bishop of Rome would be the President, he would be a Bishop among Bishops and he would recognise that his authority does not override the customs and teachings of the churches of the east. The Orthodox Bishops would then continue to exercise their present ministries. The Pope would remain as the focus of the global unity as the universal pastor, not the sole legislator. A difficult mix, certainly, but could there be some way through the tight knot of dispute? I wonder. On our side there would need to be a movement from the Pope as the sole legislative and doctrinal authority towards the Pope as the front point, the public symbol, of the church's mission and care for humanity. On your side it would mean a coming-together with recognition that Rome has a historical centrality which provides a visible symbol of our unity in Christ.

Now that's a long shot. Could it ever be possible? Could you even approach it?

If you think that there is even a glimmer of light in this, then it would be right for me, and I expect for you, to share this correspondence with colleagues to see whether there is any support for a more formal way of approach. As far as I am concerned personally, I believe that we have here a framework for an important discussion."

In all this correspondence Niki realised that Terracini was revealing the strengths and the weaknesses of the intellectual. He could see the issues with great clarity. He could understand that compromises would have to be made. He saw, in his mind, sensible, hopeful solutions to age-old problems. He could propound them with simplicity. But in all this he was forgetting the passions of a millennium and the profound attachment to tradition which was innate to the hierarchy. To move a millimetre would be a triumph. To make such major shifts would take an earthquake high on the Richter scale. He must surely be a brave man to start such a journey and must have some sort of encouragement from the Pope.

Patriarch Olav was feeling his age. Excited by the latest letter, he was able only to send a warm and appreciative reply without any commitment. Then he managed a phone connection with the ecumenical officer of the Greek Orthodox patriarch, Bishop Athenagoras, asking if he could plan a visit to Moscow for consultation on serious ecumenical affairs. This bishop was well known on the inter-church circuit. He was a tall, strong man built on the lines of a guardsman, but with a gentle humour, kind eyes and singing voice. His special ministry was in the direction of prayer and worship, for he believed that the unity of Christians was best approached, not through constitutions and creeds, but through meditation, chant, prayer, wonder and awe before God.

He agreed to the journey. He sat in Olav's library to read the whole correspondence, continually surprised, his emotions stirred, but finding it hard to believe that this was a genuine opening. In their discussion he felt bound to ask that he and Nicholas should visit Cardinal Terracini in Rome, to discern how seriously to take the letters and how best to pursue the matter in the light of the Kremlin's hostility.

***

In Geneva Walter Schwartz was eagerly following the matter, sensing that it was the biggest issue to come onto the agenda during his term of service. He did not want to be fooled by it if it should be a cul-de-sac, but neither could he afford to neglect such a glittering opportunity. He discussed it with Miriam Menzies and agreed with her that the entry of the Greek bishop showed that it was being taken seriously, so they encouraged Niki to join in a visit to the Vatican.

Walter felt that he needed to share this with Lucy, for it was such a busy agitation in his mind. She would be discreet. Since their fright over the child Eric, Lucy knew that she had to be very supportive for Walter. She knew that there was no longer any passionate sex between them and she often wondered at the meaning of love and how that was so steadily confused with passion. She had the disturbing sense that whenever they were intimate, she was also watching them from outside, assessing the words and the feelings, planning the next move. It was as though she was both the person fully engaged in the relationship and also the watcher. She felt that this was her failing, perhaps even a betrayal of love; it moved her to be ever more interested in Walter's work and more generously thoughtful for his office relationships.

Out at Bossey, Niki and Petrovna were finding that it was not always easy to live in such a community, with most of their meals in the common dining room; it meant readjustment for them both, but their presence was welcomed by staff and students for they were such an attractive and well-informed couple, opening the Russian dimension of the church to the Asians and Africans who had never met it before. Petrovna soon came to know the Blue Angels as individuals, understood those who were homesick and counselled the flighty ones who imagined they were in Switzerland to indulge in exotic affairs. She was anxious to pursue their hope of adoption. Her ideas about this were clear, that it would be a Russian baby, that it would be her child, filling the great gap in their marriage.

"I don't think it has to be that way," said Niki, "for there are other opportunities here in Geneva, and I think the Swiss laws might be much stronger than those in Moscow, more certain to hold. I'm a bit suspicious of Moscow lawyers."

"But what babies are likely to be available for adoption here?"

"I would like to go to the Red Cross and see if we could adopt a baby from a refugee camp. I've heard that they really need adopting parents quite desperately."

"No, Niki, then it would not be a Russian baby. It would probably be African. Then always a stranger, an outsider in Russia and never my very own child."

"We could be doing something important, dear, helping to break down the barriers. It would be like our own way to deal with racism."

"But that's not what adoption is about, Niki. It is about us, our marriage, our life together, not about international politics. Please don't let this come between us."

"No, never that. Let us just think about it for a few days. You know that you are very precious to me and it must be right for both of us."

Niki was not oppressed with the sense of being childless, for he was caught up in the big problems and hopes of his work; they filled his mind. He sensed that his initial work as the courier for the correspondence between Cardinal and Patriarch was ending, that it was being taken to a higher level which would be discussed in Rome when he and Bishop Athenagoras were to meet with the Cardinal.

They were received with great politeness in the offices of the Secretariat for Christian Unity and ushered into the Cardinal's study. Introductions were made, senior staff introduced, coffee served and then they settled down to talk.

"I am sure, Bishop, that you have read the correspondence with the dear Patriarch and you will be wondering how seriously to take it. Is it just a flight of fancy by me, a dreamer, and without any hope of reality? That question must be in your mind."

"Yes, your Grace, of course it is. These thousand years of separation between us are such a heavy weight. There are very suspicious people on both sides. We all have conservative colleagues who would fight changes. So of course I wonder how seriously to take the letters."

"I am ready to answer you. This office of the Catholic Church is serious. We have been thinking about this for years, and especially since there have been such bad relationships in the Ukraine and some violent episodes. We have looked at it as a challenge to do something practical towards reconciliation by the end of this millennium, for a thousand years of excommunication is surely long enough. There must be ways through the minefield."

"That is very reassuring and hopeful. But it may still be that you are speaking for a small element of the Church."

"I am ready to share with you what has been hidden from Nicholas and the Patriarch. In half an hour we are to have a meeting with the Holy Father so that you will know his mind."

"That is the best news, and whether Pope Gregory is in favour of this movement or not, it will be the greatest help in deciding how the Orthodox should respond."

Terracini and his senior assistant then led the Bishop and Nicholas across the courtyard and into the papal apartments, up the stairs and into the private office, where the Pope's secretary welcomed them.

The door opened and Gregory came forward, embraced them and led them into his study. He was now 74 years old, a slight figure in white, a kindly smile, glasses with thick lenses, a remarkable memory for people, and a mind of his own. Now into the fifth year of his papacy he was hopeful that the system would not imprison him, for he had outlived some of the more officious of the papal advisors.

"You are most welcome, Bishop and Archdeacon, as we explore this adventure which my dear ecumenical Cardinal has in mind. I have to tell you that the correspondence, which was his personal initiative, has had my full knowledge and backing. It must be according to the Divine will for us to seek reconciliation with all who love God and follow our Lord. It is a mighty challenge. If there is only one thing that I can achieve in this office, it would be to start the movement to heal the two great breaches in fellowship, that of one thousand years ago with the Orthodox and the one five hundred years ago with the children of the Reformation. Of course, I know that in my time we might not get very far. But there has to be a first step. And I am prepared to take it."

"Your Holiness, these words are like sunshine on a dark day. You are taking this matter to your heart. We know how slowly the churches move. The tortoise is speedy compared with the Orthodox. But if we could together take that first step then I believe it would be very hard for the Metropolitans of the Orthodox to resist joining in the journey. We would have to give them a sign of hope, that arguments will not be infinite and that we deal with the realities of the people of God."

'Well, Bishop, you have seen in the correspondence that there is, here in the Vatican, some sense of movement, some readiness for change. I know that there will be many conservatives who will object to this. We won't be all of one mind. But if I can give a clear signal, a signal that is firmly based on Catholic understanding of scripture, I believe that most of the Church will be eager to come with me, and those who are not eager will endure it"

"This is now becoming too great a matter for a one-to-one correspondence, Your Holiness. Among the Orthodox there will have to be senior support for it. That will mean that it will become a public matter. Are you prepared for that?"

"Yes, I have thought about that. My suggestion is that the dialogue between us be officially inaugurated at a meeting with full public coverage, so that nobody can speak of secret deals. Cardinal, I would expect you to gather eight or ten of the senior colleagues to be with you at the meeting, and I hope you, Bishop, might do the same. I would be there to open the meeting."

"But I do not think it would be wise to have the meeting here, Your Holiness. That might be interpreted as though we were coming as suppliants to beg for recognition."

"No, you are quite right, Bishop. Nor should we think of Geneva or Moscow or Athens. There is only one place that would surely be right for such an enterprise – Istanbul, which I still think of as Constantinople. That was where the papal envoys declared the final separation a thousand years ago, and that is where the first step towards healing should take place. I will be ready to go there next April at Easter. With that as the target, can you, on both sides, organise a major event with good preparatory materials? You will need to engage the security people and the media, but do that with care, for remember that this will be the inauguration, not the achievement. Bishop, I am asking you to explore, with your colleagues, the best location in the city for the meeting. Now, with such a vision in our minds, let us go into my little chapel and pray."

He led them to the simple chapel, where they knelt in silence. The candle lighted the cross. Niki was deeply moved. After some minutes, the Pope prayed, "You know our hearts, Lord God. Take from us all personal ambition in what we are planning. Help us to know your will. Guide us with your Spirit. Lead us towards the unity of your people. Our Father...."

In a swirl of emotions – excitement, surprise, anxiety – they went back with the knowledge that a great deal of very hard and detailed work was ahead. It would be their full-time task for the next six months. It was the opportunity of a lifetime.

***

The first announcement came on Vatican radio. His Holiness would be visiting Istanbul next Easter to show fraternal respect for the Orthodox churches. Next summer he planned to visit Germany, Belgium and the Netherlands... The report was not taken up widely but was noted in the Kremlin.

'There you are," stormed Yumin, "I knew something was going on. I told you. The Vatican people are going to pose as the friends of the Orthodox. It's all a political thing. You can see the hand of America in it. The Americans will fund the Catholics to cause trouble, setting the church against us all across Europe. You're responsible for state security, Semilov, can't you see what's happening?"

"I can see that there is some unrest in Hungary and Poland, but my people say that this latest news is just a religious thing. They have not found any political pressures in it. No, sir, the main problems we are facing are in the Caucasus, these independence movements. They are the threat to the unity of the nation. And they are not easy to deal with."

"You mean you cannot crush them in the old way?"

"We could crush the leadership people, but the movements are popular, others would fill the vacant spots. People are saying that in Georgia it's like the Congress in India and the British, or like Ho Chi Min and the French. We can police the place, we can put a lid on the noise, but we cannot control five million thoughts."

"Are you becoming a bit soft?"

"No, sir, but I have learnt after many years to be realistic."

"Well, your people bungled the Olav matter. That was bad management."

Dissension was in the air. Yumin began to wonder about his own position with the comrades, for they seemed to be more critical than they had dared to be before. Like emperors and prime ministers who are unsure of the loyalty of their courtiers and parties, Yumin was beginning to see dangerous shadows at every corner. He was not sure how much he was being told, how much was hidden from him. He was sure that now, as in all the decades of its life, the Soviet Union faced genuine dangers, but he was puzzled – was it still the United States, was it internal? Could it be the economic pressure? Was the army still fully under political control? Could it be trusted? And now this religious thing too.

In the pit the bear glared at the moving, shouting figures, wondering which of them held the steel-tipped prod.

***

As soon as he returned to Geneva, Niki reported to Walter and Miriam the exciting news of the initiative of the Pope. They could see that, for the first time, there might be some possibility of movement in the historic pattern of separation, and for this they could only give thanks. Ecumenism would take new life and hope.

"Of course, we cannot assume either speed or success," said Niki, "but we should surely welcome such a new move. The Pope was fully aware of the issues and plainly had this plan in his mind for a while."

"For Faith and Order," Miriam was clear, "it means that we should prepare to meet any proposal for talks in a more concerted way so that there could be one conversation rather than a dozen. We might begin to talk with the world communions about that. It's quite a list, you know, the Anglican communion, the Lutheran family, the Presbyterian and Reformed family, the Methodist World body, the Baptists, the Moravians, the Disciples and more."

"Don't press it too hard at this early stage," advised Walter, "for it may be a long trail. I suggest that you might just take some informal soundings as this news gradually hits the religious press. I think it also means the end of the private correspondence we have been dealing with, just as soon as the preparations for next Easter are publicised. Then it will be direct contact between the heads of the two offices; possibly they will set up a joint office to do the planning."

"If the Orthodox ask me to join in that planning, what would you advise me to do?"

"Let us face that if it comes, Nicholas. I think we should continue with our work with our present agendas; there is plenty to do."

That was not easy. Niki had in his mind the Pope's study and the broad vision that he had shared. Beside that the daily business of encouraging the evangelical fringe churches to have some thought for unity and listening to the pains of conservatives who objected to the ordination of women in the Church of England and helping to shape the liturgy for a common celebration of Pentecost – it all seemed verging on the trivial. His unease continued at home with Petrovna.

"Niki, I really want to move on from this stay in Bossey. It's not that I am unhappy here but I need something more than this. Can't we look forward now to a settled home and a child?"

"I hope so, my dear. But it's hard to see the future."

"Well, we can plan the future. We're not puppets."

"I am in the service of the church and I believe that is where I ought to be. So we have to ask where the church calls me to work. Geneva has been an education for me. I've learnt so much about the whole community and I think I've been useful. But perhaps now it would be a good time to ask the Patriarch what he has in mind for us."

"If you can do that then let us ask for a posting in Russia so that we can go ahead with an adoption there. That's what is important for me."

Niki had no heart for an extended argument about this. He organised a phone call from his office to Moscow to sound out the Patriarch, explaining that there were domestic matters as well as big policy to have in mind, and asking where his continued service might best be located. Olav was very ready to answer and had plainly been discussing this with his counsellors and with other Metropolitans.

"You have being doing well for us in Geneva and that is appreciated. All that work has now to be reshaped with this initiative of Pope Gregory. It seems to us that for the next period there will be a heavy load of work leading to next Easter at Istanbul. We are ready to set up our Russian office in the Crimea at Simferopol, the Greek church group will be in Athens, and the joint committee may meet in Istanbul at the Ecumenical Patriarchate, with the Catholics flying in from Rome. We want you to head the small office in the Crimea. I am writing to Walter Schwarz in Geneva to ask that you be released to undertake this vital work. How does that sound to you?"

It sounded very well to Niki and delighted Petrovna, who could see a proper home life opening up ahead. A month later there was a farewell party for them at Bossey and then one in the Geneva office, where Petrovna was surprised at the number of senior people who wanted to thank Niki for his service. Walter Schwarz spoke for them all when he said that Niki had been such a good colleague, he wanted to ensure that he was followed by another gift of service from the Orthodox.

"What you will be doing is important for us all. So please keep in touch as often as possible. Miriam, you will taking over the Joint Committee work, which will now have a different focus. No more small issues. You will have to prepare to face the great Reformation issues – scripture and tradition, the nature of the church, the individual conscience and the unity of the body, the grace of God and the priesthood of all believers – How I would like us to be able to concentrate all our resources on these things. You see Niki, that while you are facing one set of divisive factors, we here will have to concentrate on these others if we are to be partners with the Vatican in a serious attempt. I fancy that we are both starting out on long roads and we may not live to see the end. But here's to your new office and your new home. Our thanks go with you, thanks also to Petrovna who has been a marvellous influence in the Bossey community."

Their small collection of personal belongings was soon parcelled and boxed and sent on its long train journey, with, thought Petrovna, a fifty-fifty chance of arriving at Simferopol. The Russian train and station staff were renowned for misdirecting, mislaying, purloining and damaging luggage; you could either bribe or pray. Their personal journey was by air. Neither had been in the Crimea before, so they looked around at the airport and the drive into the city to get a clue to the nature of the place. It seemed grey and dusty. There was plenty of the grim Soviet architecture, the apartment blocks which blighted every Russian city. But it became much more interesting in the centre where some of the older buildings remained, the squares were graced with trees where, in summer, there would be sidewalk cafes. The cathedral and the bishop's house were in the old centre of town, an impressive and rather ornate group of buildings, looking a little tired. At the house the couple were met at the entrance by the housekeeper, Mrs Rubetz, stern, grey-haired, built on the four square pattern with girth almost equal to height.

"We will go in to meet the bishop in a minute but first let me take you to the office which will be the workplace for the planning group. We have been cleaning it up for you."

They walked round to the rear garden where there was a cottage, formerly used by the church counselling service and before that by the family of the gardener. It was newly painted. There were three rooms, one large enough for meetings, with one of the old stoves in the corner, large enough to warm the whole place. In one room there were two large filing cabinets and a gas ring for boiling the kettle.

"This is Timoteo Tachek, who will be your assistant and clerk."

Mrs Rubetz introduced the young man, a thin figure, but evidently very efficient at office routines and communications. They went back into the main house to meet Bishop Konstantin, who was in his fifties, a man who enjoyed life, who told good stories and was appreciated throughout the Crimea diocese as "so easy to talk to" and "he's a cleric who understands life."

"You are both very welcome. You see that we have begun to make ready for your work here Nicholas, for we know it is work that is important for us all and that you are recommended to us by the Moscow Patriarch. Don't hesitate to come direct to me if there is anything you need. Early morning is good time to catch me. Now you will be tired after the journey and it is time that you see your new home. My driver will take you. You will need a car, I think, and we can buy a second hand small car. The house has basic furnishing and you are free to add anything personal. And don't be frightened by Mrs Rubetz here. I know she looks sternly at the world but you will find her a bundle of good sense and total reliability."

Their house was on the outskirts of the town, with a garden, the ground floor built of stone and an upper floor, which looked as though it had been added later, built entirely of timber, with two bedrooms. The bishop's driver went around switching on lights and unlocking doors to show them that everything was in working order, and he brought in their baggage. He said he would call for Niki at 8.30 next morning and then left them to their own devices. They explored together. They could have been critical of the paint on the walls and the roughness of the kitchen floor, but they were so delighted to have this house of their own that they ignored the defects. Petrovna was excited to have some garden she could develop. Mrs Rubetz had provided basic food in the kitchen cupboard and the refrigerator. They looked along the street, lined with trees, now leafless but with buds glistening in the shafts of bright sunlight between showers.

In the next days, Niki learnt how the work might be handled. The supervision of this Russian Orthodox share in the dialogue with the Vatican would be undertaken by Archbishop Stanislav of Kiev and there would be correspondence with other senior clergy in order to reach a common position on all the delicate issues. Niki would go to Istanbul where the various Orthodox churches would come together, for the Romanians, Bulgarians, Serbians, Syrians as well as the Greeks would need to share in the party. Timoteo Tachek proved to have a comprehensive address file and knew the right time to make phone calls to distant places, with the patience to put them through. He also brewed the frequent cups of tea required for greeting visitors.

While this was going on, Petrovna knew her priority. She called a taxi to take her to the Municipal Offices, where she asked for the legal department. There she waited. It was a long wait, but eventually she reached the enquiries desk and asked for copies of the forms needed to apply for an adoption order. That meant passing her on to another department and another wait. Eventually, by late afternoon, she had the forms and could read a summary of the process. She looked at the listing of adoption agencies and decided to try first the diocesan orphanage, for that seemed a natural first call. She went home and showed the papers to Niki that evening.

"My, you're a fast worker, dear."

"Well, I can't see any point in waiting for we don't know how long this process is going to take. If it is typically Russian, we might be on the end of a long queue."

"Perhaps we put in applications to several agencies. But you are surely right to put the church orphanage first because we might get a special fast track there."

"I hope the cases arrive at the station soon so that we can have our own kitchen things and bedlinen and towels. Is there any way to check?"

"I'm not sure but I can go to the station tomorrow and ask."

"And you must follow up the Bishop's offer of a car, for surely he won't send his driver every day, and the busses don't seem very frequent."

Niki was impressed and a little scared by Petrovna's efficiency, for there seemed too much to do so quickly. He had to make the office work and meet many people and be prepared to travel while being fully involved in the great desire to adopt a child. In his heart he knew that her priorities were right and that they should adopt while they were still young but, like an expectant father, he wondered if he could meet her expectations.

6

For the first time in a generation the Ecumenical Patriarch in Istanbul was courted by the government and the media. Normally he was disregarded by the powers, secure in their Moslem majority and their Turkish nationalism, but now he was invited to the government's inner sanctum to discuss how to cope with a papal visit. The first question, as it is so often, was who would pay the expenses of security and hospitality. Ankara claimed that security was their concern and they would pay that bill; it would an honour for the state. The city, expecting a windfall of tourist income, offered to book and pay for a hotel for the Rome party. The rest, the food, the trips and outings, the translators, the medical back-up and the transport around the city would be left for the Patriarch to meet. In his discreet and often forgotten corner of the old city, the Patriarch knew that he had no funds to meet such costs, so would have to rely on contacts and generosity.

But there was one issue which he was ready to press.

"You know that the Pope is coming to inaugurate a fresh dialogue with us in a search for reconciliation. I have been thinking that there is only one place where the key meeting should happen and that is Hagia Sophia. A thousand years ago that is where the papal legates came with the documents of excommunication. I know the building is now a public space as a museum, but I am asking that for two or three days it be closed for that purpose and set up for this very special meeting. Can you do that?"

"That is asking a lot. All the tourists come here expecting that they can visit that building. To close it would cause great disappointment and also loss of revenue."

"But it has often been closed for redecorations and repairs."

"Agreed, but we only did that for the sake of public safety."

"How would it be if we ensured that, at the rear, there were seats for the public, with a first come first seated basis, and a careful security screening. Then we could say that the building has not been closed."

"I think that could work. Let's find out the dates from the Vatican."

So the stage was set. In the great, cavernous space, impressive and smelling of history, it seemed almost beyond modern imagination to see it as a church. The Patriarch, a small man, felt even smaller as he looked up at the great dome. Like the Pantheon in Rome, it breathed an antique worship. But there it stood and for one more day in its life it would become the focus of the world's Christian people. The media people will want a lot more light, he thought. In another way it is surely right, for the history and the scale of it makes all our human struggles and doubts and pains seem but temporary, to be taken in our stride, for we are not such impressive people. What can we build?

His next priority was to call Bishop Athenagoras in Athens and Nicholas in the Crimea to come for a discussion on the programme for the event, the invitation list, the liturgical elements and the speakers. They would then ask the Cardinal in Rome to send his representatives to Istanbul to seek agreement on the whole schedule.

The first attempt at a programme proved to be remarkably straightforward. There would be three days to schedule.

Day 1 Informal The Pope would have some time to relax. There would be a boat trip to view the Bosphorus, a landing to see the site of Scutari, to sail along the Golden Horn and a fish lunch with locals. In the evening the city would host a dinner.

Day 2 Liturgical Morning Prayers, Orthodox. Service of Penitence in the afternoon. Catholic led service of Preparation for a new Relationship in the evening. At three different local churches.

Day 3 In St Sophia, with the members of the Incoming Relationship Committee in a special position. A large choir. In the chairs on the platform 10 senior figures from each tradition – seated for the opening as two separate groups but after the speeches to mingle, interwoven. The Pope and the Ecumenical Patriarch central. Just those two speeches. Then a hymn or chant from each tradition. Then the dedication of the incoming special committee members.

They thought that this third day should ideally be Holy Thursday so that John 17 could be read on the actual day of the Last Supper; that would set the tone for all discussion of the unity of Christians.

"Well," said Athenagoras, "that will give them something to think about. I hope we can keep plenty of time for people to be quiet and pray without words. That's important to me."

"How would it be," suggested Niki, "if the main meeting opens with fifteen minutes of silent prayer, perhaps with some quiet music, and each person stands or kneels according to tradition. The media would not like that, but we must forget them if we are to do justice to the spirit of the occasion."

The Vatican response was warmly approving but made the suggestion that the Pope would wish to have some occasion for a friendly meeting with Islamic leaders. This called for diplomacy, as there was a rising tide of traditional Islam in the political machinery of Turkey, and little respect for the remnants of ancient Christianity in this, one of its earliest homes. The Moslem leadership in Istanbul proved more ready to entertain the Pope than the more conservative Imams in Ankara, and so it was arranged – a lunch on the second day for a small number of guests and an hour to talk after the meal.

In his Crimea office, Niki was responsible for sharing the plans with the senior officers of the Russian church. At home, with Petrovna, the adoption forms were signed and the orphanage visited. The matron spoke of the need for good adopting parents, examined their records and said that they would be high on the list. It all depended on the number of babies that were placed in their care, but probably the call would come within a month.

Petrovna was delighted with this news and began to haunt the shops in town to see what baby needs could be met. It was going to be a strain on their stipend but worth making sacrifices for. Soon the second bedroom was repainted, a cot installed and a pile of towelling nappies filled the bottom drawer. Petrovna took it as a remarkable sign that one morning early in spring, the patch of lawn, untidy at the end of the hard winter, blossomed with a crowd of tiny purple blooms, little tulips, each no larger than your thumb, each with a yellow centre. The railway had at last delivered their cases. All seemed battered but largely intact and the house took on a more friendly look as they hung their few pictures and put down their colourful rugs.

The orphanage call came at the beginning of Lent. They ran out to the car and drove at rather reckless speed right across the city, up the driveway to the doors of the severe old building. The matron smiled to see them, so eager, "You must have flown here." She called a nurse and soon there she was, fast asleep in the nurse's arms, a tiny bundle, well wrapped, dark hair, pale skin, perfect little ears and a snub nose.

"Please sit down and let me tell you about Katrina. We have called her Katrina, but you may register her under another name if you wish. We have to make sure that the mother fully understands what she is doing when she brings a baby to us. In this case we were fully satisfied that the mother could not care for her child, her circumstances – which I cannot disclose – made it impossible. And she had no knowledge of the whereabouts of the father, no contact at all. As far as we could tell, there were no adverse medical signs in either the mother or in Katrina. The baby seems quite normal and healthy. But she needs care. Are you now ready to give that care, not just for a few months, but for the rest of your lives? That is the big question which you have been thinking about, and this is your last chance to say Yes or No."

"We say Yes. This has been our firm intention and our prayer."

"Then go with Katrina and a blessing." The matron stood up and made the sign of the cross over the baby and kissed her. Petrovna received this most precious bundle and suddenly appeared in the starring role of mother, as though this was the part for which nature had designed her from childhood, fulfilling her emotional life and bringing a fresh sparkle to her eyes. They drove home more carefully.

Katrina opened her eyes and yawned. Soon Petrovna had a bottle ready and warm. Niki was quickly taking photos from every angle, impressed with the new model of his lovely wife and determined to do his best as a nervous father. Nappie duty had to be learnt. Bureaucracy had to be dealt with, registration, adoption orders, medical checks.

A slight hitch occurred at that point when the hospital looked up their records, to find that the papers sent on from Geneva were all in French, which the local hospital clerks could not translate. Petrovna translated for them, only to become aware that she had missed her six-monthly check-up, now three months overdue. She skipped over that; surely nothing was wrong and there was no need to get into a fresh medical process at the very time when she had a baby to care for. So the hospital gave them all the right ticks and the formalities were completed. They kept the name Katrina.

Niki told Bishop Konstantin the whole story, the household celebrated and planned the baptism in the cathedral. Petrovna's mother flew from Moscow for the event, determined to be present although nervous at leaving her flat empty. Messages were sent to Miriam and Walter in Geneva and to Olav in Moscow, so that many could share the happiness of the couple. Baptism in the Othodox was a serious matter. No mere sprinkling but whole bathing in the font was necessary, Katrina yelling in outrage, the bishop then cuddling the noisy bundle in warm blankets until a hint of a smile appeared, and joyfully handing the baby back to her mother. Lunch was provided by the bishop with bottles of the best local red wine for the toasts.

***

In Geneva Miriam Menzies was seeking to gather support for a concerted response to the papal initiative, no small task with such disparate bodies, each with its own traditions and emphases. There were many earlier documents on which to build. Anglicans had had long discussions with Catholics, so had Lutherans, and their reports were scholarly and too academic in style to be widely read. Miriam wrote to all the world communions, pleading that they could only respond effectively by doing the work together; it was only if that effort failed that they should go back to separate channels of communication with Rome.

"Let us be positive," she wrote, "and recognise that a great deal of the folly and corruption which the great Reformers found in Rome, have long been dealt with. The list of old causes for separation does not hold today. Therefore we need to be clear as to the barriers to full fellowship which we still recognise, to state why these things are important to us, and to suggest how they might be overcome. If we can do this together then we can meet the papal initiative with hope."

She invited the leaders of the world communions to come to Geneva for a two day meeting in order to sort out the key issues. After writing the preparatory paper, she took it to Walter to ensure that he was kept will informed.

"This is all very clear, Miriam, and the issues are the key ones – the authority of the Bible and the place of tradition, the calling of the priesthood and the laity, the room for diversity within the unity of the whole, the place of women, and the authority of the Pope. My only hesitation about this is that if the whole effort comes to nothing, then we as a Council will carry the burden of failure. It is quite a risk."

"But, Walter, we can only live by taking risks. If we just let things slide along the old way then we can be sure that no real progress will be made. This way we have at least a chance of doing something worthwhile for the whole ecumenical movement. I think the Pope is taking a very considerable risk when he goes to Istanbul. We must not creep into our shell."

***

As the ice broke up on the Moscow river, a reception was held in the St George's Hall in the Kremlin, a splendid space shining in white and gold, where the members of the Central Committee of the Party were enjoying drinks after their long annual session. They gathered in corners to discuss the balance of influence, the promotion of some who had spoken well and the slow dismissal of old warriors, the strength of the military group and the muddled leadership of Yumin, who had seemed indecisive on all the controversial matters.

He was a leader who had lost his central conviction, who had no guiding star, who met each challenge with uneasy pragmatism and so inspired nobody.

A group of members stood around him; he was unsure which of them he could trust. A younger member said, "Mr President, I think you must be tired after all that business."

"Not at all. I feel fine."

"But a little holiday might be just right," an army general agreed.

"Yes, Mr President, we think that our young friend is correct. A holiday is overdue. We have a concern for your welfare. We have arranged a special flight and a splendid villa in Odessa. You will be collected at 11.0 pm tonight and taken to the airport where the Air Force will look after you. We have ensured that the very best medical and kitchen staff will be there, so you should enjoy a break from the Moscow climate."

Yumin looked round at their closed faces. He could not think of any way out, for he had no idea whether the police or the army would back him.

"I need some time to pass on urgent business matters to a deputy who can act while I am away."

"That won't be necessary. Marshal Rubetsky here has been following matters closely and will stand in for you very competently."

"But he is not my choice."

"It is the clear majority view of the Central Committee, and you will, of course, accept it."

He was escorted from the hall. A motor cycle police escort was waiting. He was seen into his limousine by three army officers. They sped through cleared streets to his impressive old mansion where the officers entered with him and stayed while his valet packed his suitcases. It had all been well planned so that, at every moment, he was being 'helped' to depart. In full public view the President had been coldly and clinically disempowered, no guns, no shouting, but as fatally stabbed as Caesar on the Ides of March.

Next morning the papers led with the story that because of exhaustion, the President had departed for a holiday, and his place was being taken by Marshal Rubetsky, a 55 year old staff officer with a sound grasp of strategy, a sketchy knowledge of economics and considerable self-regard. He looked forward to dealing with presidents and prime ministers. His conviction was that the Soviet Union must modernise, that this was urgent in order to compete in the modern world, and that it should be done with compulsion if necessary. The members of the Central Committee were of one mind in supporting this priority. Communications had to be improved – telephone and television, road and rail, airports and planes – if the vast country was to act as one nation. Some individual enterprise seemed to be essential to improve the torpid economy; this would be encouraged in agriculture first and then in retail and then in manufacturing, the State holding the natural resources. Whether this would be enough to meet the expectations of millions, time would tell.

***

In Istanbul, a great Moslem city, the excitement of the Pope's arrival was not as fervent as in most of his visits, but there was a formal guard of honour at the airport, the Prime Minister and cabinet members, a military band and a fine length of red carpet. All due honour was offered but there was no kneeling to kiss the ring. The Excelsior Hotel was secluded in a garden, the trees shining in new green, the army patrolling, the suites luxurious and the hosts attentive. The Patriarch arrived to greet the Pope and share any questions about the programme. As they faced each other across the coffee table, each looked for hope and each remembered the long history which would be the drag on progress. Both men represented millions of faithful Christians, many of whom wanted nothing in their religion to change - the ancient prayers and rituals, the old chants, the same approach to the same altar, the same round of holy days and the same old sermons. But both were sensitive enough to realise that religious monoliths would be hard pushed to meet a world of rising material expectations, a world of scientific wonders, a world of dangerous nationalisms, a world where old authority was melting as the ice of winter in spring sunshine. History must be put in its place.

Gregory and his entourage were embarked on a ferry for the trip to view the grandeurs of the seaway, with the fabled domes and minarets of the old city a photographer's joy. History shaped the place, history was what formed its story and wealth and sorrow. Geography made it the bridge between Europe and Asia; history coloured it with blood and gold. The new high-rise buildings were intrusive, like flourishing weeds in the garden. So, as they settled in the saloon for a fish lunch, Gregory thought of the power of our histories, both drag and inspiration. But the people invited to sit with the Pope at lunch were fishermen and their wives, not philosophers, and the conversation – a slow process with interpreters - was about family life and childhood and educational opportunities and the scarcity of the finest fish and the cost of boat maintenance.

"Here we are going to great lengths to deal with the broken relationships of the church of God," thought Gregory, "when these people, and people like them everywhere, just want some assurance, some relief from worry, and hope for their children. They want a blessing now, not just in paradise. We must not get too far apart from their concerns. I must look at my speech again."

**

Thursday morning at St Sophia. A platform laid with blue carpet. A table covered with white and gold damask. Rows of chairs under the television lights. And the vast space above disappearing into the dark. To one side the Orthodox choir of two hundred who were to sing a capella, and on the other side the members of the proposed Relationship Council. Distinguished guests in the front seats facing the platform included the Archbishop of Canterbury and the heads a many Reformed churches, the ambassadors from the diplomatic missions in Ankara and nuns and monks from all the main Catholic religious communities.

A deep choir chant began and the two processions, splendid in their festal robes, moved from the rear up the two aisles, to their seats on the platform with the Patriarch and Pope in the centre. On the Patriarch's side, all was green and gold, on the Pope's side purple and white.

Everyone was standing. The Patriarch spoke, "Today we come on a holy day to begin a holy task. We have no other way in which to begin than to pray to our Lord and to place ourselves under the authority of the Holy Spirit, that we may be obedient to his will. We pray first in silence." At that, the party of the platform turned around to face the large screen behind the platform which showed the Leonardo fresco of the Last Supper. The silence, a thousand people hushed and intent, was prolonged. Then, suddenly, a commotion. At the rear, among the public seating, three people were shouting, screaming. The words were indistinct but echoing around the ancient walls, "Changement jamais." That seemed to be the theme. Police surrounded the three, hustled them roughly away, still shouting, ran them out of the building and into a police van. They turned out to be members of an ultra-conservative French Catholic movement. It was a moment of nervous shock, threatening the careful introduction of the service.

"Let us listen now," the Patriarch kept his voice slow and steady, "to the holy Gospel."

The procession of the Word moved up to the platform, a young man holding aloft a 6th century copy of the Gospels. The passage from John 17, the prayer of Jesus for the unity of his followers, was read by a Benedictine nun.

At last everyone could sit down. The choir chanted a Psalm. A Metropolitan prayed. Then the Pope stood.

"I greet you all in the name and in the spirit of the Christ who prayed for the unity of all his disciples. I greet all the representatives of the Government of the Republic and of this city who have received us so generously. I give thanks to all who have prepared the way for us. We are here today to remember history and to make history. We remember the Last Supper, the table of God's grace in Christ, at which the church has been fed for two millennia, the memory becoming the food for pilgrims through the ages. We come also to remember the events of a thousand years ago when the legates of the pope came here and laid on the holy table the edict of excommunication of the Patriarch and his followers. That was the culmination of many years of dispute and much bitterness. On all sides we have to make confession for so great a sorrow.

I am very aware that such a history cannot be undone, washed away, for it has become part of us. As you see us here today, you recognise that we are people shaped by our predecessors, who were, in their day, as learned, faithful and devout as any of us. But the grace of God brings to us, in this generation, a word which we are called to hear, and that word which has been given to me is 'reconciliation'.

It is a word for the whole church of God, that we should find reconciliation with one another as sisters and brothers with a common love of the Lord Jesus Christ. It is a word which millions of people long to hear, all who live in the shadows of war, where death is violent, and all who are separated by tribal or cultural loyalties, and all who know the pain of a broken marriage. We pray today that reconciliation might be the blessing for the church and for the world.

Those of us who come here today from Rome know well that we are beginning a difficult journey and that success is not assured, for there are genuine obstacles to overcome, genuine beliefs which we cannot dismiss. It is not only in theology that we have to seek a common mind, but in ethics, which may prove even more testing. Teaching and practice have to walk hand in hand. We shall need to enter into each other's experience and learn from each other's way of holiness.

Today we cannot see the end of the journey. The Gospels do not reveal to us the constitution or the global pattern of the church. Indeed it may well be true that unity is not the end but the journey itself, a constant movement in obedience to the Spirit, never completed, always demanding confession and renewal. But because we do not see the end, we cannot fail to attempt the journey. I am here today to pledge that we will begin and continue this journey with full hope and serious intent, to reverse that edict of a thousand years ago, and find a fresh unity between these two great families of faith. We pray to the Lord for wisdom, patience and love, and we ask all faithful people to pray with us.

The risen Christ approached his followers with the word 'Shalom', which means peace, peace in our hearts, peace in our homes, peace for the nations and peace for the church. In this splendid shrine, and in this great company, I say to the faithful people of all the Orthodox churches, in the Spirit of Christ, Shalom."

There was applause as the Pope sat down, a sense that something remarkable was happening, and immediately the Patriarch rose to respond.

"Your Holiness, you come to us with that word of grace. We respond to you with thanksgiving, that you have chosen this message on this day to open a fresh page of our history. Our Orthodox churches have been through great trials, our people have known suffering, in poverty and oppression, through the centuries. In this very city blood has stained every patch of soil. So history has made us cautious and perhaps defensive.

Now we are called to open our hearts to you, to share our living faith with you. We do so gladly. Our people will share in the Reconciliation Council with eagerness and with realism. They know it will not be easy, for they will have to carry our faithful people with them. But we have already seen signs of hope in some of the preliminary work that has been done, and more particularly in your presence and your words today.

I wish to request the Council to set as a practice that they publish on this Holy Thursday every year a report on their progress, telling us all of their themes and their agreements, so that there is nothing secret or private but all is declared for the churches to read. I believe this is essential if we are ever to carry the great mass of our people with us on the journey.

Then I wish to ask that no questions are closed questions. If there are tough issues, let them be faced. And they must be faced together in prayer. Sometimes it is our quietness which allows the wind of the Spirit to speak to us.

So we launch this boat, as they say when they launch a ship, "God bless her and all who sail in her." May we be guided and heartened by the God of Grace. May our sins be forgiven and may God's will be done."

The choir rose to sing the Magnificat. During the singing the clergy on the platform got up from their seats and started to change places so that the two quite separate groups were mingled, a Catholic sitting next to an Orthodox; a splendid melange of colour. Then the members of the new Reconciliation Council stood before the platform. Niki was there and Terracini, conscious that they had helped to bring about this event and thankful that so far hope was fulfilled. The Patriarch, speaking in Greek, and the Pope, in Latin, charged them with their task, to be patient and persistent, to be generous and kind, to seek truth and unity, and to remember the life of the humblest people of the churches.

Then young people from universities and seminaries led prayers for the church and the world, ending with the Lord's Prayer which was said in a dozen languages. There was much embracing and kissing as the peace was shared. The choir sang the Gloria. Processions were reformed, a little untidily. The blessing was given by the Patriarch and Pope in unison. Trumpets called from the forecourt. The crowd slowly filed out into brilliant sunshine, as the official cars queued to carry the principal guests to a late lunch.

***

The thirty members of the Reconciliation Council stayed together for an informal meeting, getting to know one another and scheduling their first series of meetings, one in Athens and one in Rome. Niki suggested that there might be a benefit in a meeting on neutral ground and offered Bossey. This turned out to be so popular with the members that it was the most used venue in the following years. Niki was then able to catch a flight home. There he found that Petrovna was having a difficult time with Katrina who was teething and not sleeping well. Tired and feeling lonely, she listened with only half an ear to all Niki wanted to share about his great experience in Istanbul and did not respond easily to his deep sense of fulfilment. They embraced with tenderness rather than passion, sensing, for the first time, a little distance between them.

It was Petrovna who knew the real problem. She had quickly arranged for a medical check, not at the recommended six month interval, but as soon as she could after the adoption, when a neighbour offered to look after Katrina for the morning. The specialist was thorough and a little disturbed by some loss of weight – Petrovna admitted that she had had to tighten the belt on her skirts – so there were blood tests and many questions, but there was no sure evidence of trouble, just a requirement to return in three months.

Now that time had come and she was nervous, for she was not feeling as fit as she had been all her life. They all drove to the office, where they left Katrina in the care of Mrs Rubetz, then drove to the hospital. The first interview was with a physician who checked all the usual signs of physical wellbeing, and then with the oncologist who probed the possible spread of malignant cells from the original cyst. This time the report was no longer ambiguous but clear, that there was a spread of the cancer to the lymphatic system. A treatment regime was proposed. They wished that they were back in Geneva where the medical resources seemed to be more advanced, but the Russian staff were briskly efficient, no-nonsense people, and they had to be content with that.

Attentive, careful and fearful, Niki did his best to give more time to the needs at home as Bishop Konstantin assured him that hours in the office were flexible. He was able to do some of the regular shopping on the way home from the office. But what had changed most was his feeling for Petrovna. In one day she had changed from the sexually appealing woman whom he loved to touch and hold, to being a patient, apart, to be cherished and admired. This new look was both unfounded and inevitable. Petrovna had not suddenly acquired a different persona. The cancer had not yet dominated her being. She still wanted Niki as her man, easy and laughing. But it was the word, the thought, the danger that filled his mind as he washed the nappies and hung them out in the warming sunshine.

***

Miriam Menzies, who had squeezed into the public seats in St Sophia, and Walter Schwartz, who was given VIP treatment, shared the flight back to Geneva, both thinking of the implications of the great day.

"I can't see how it is going to work," said Walter, "for at the heart of it is the authority of the Pope and I can't see how that is going to be amended or reformed or shaken at all."

"I suppose Gregory must have some notion of how it might happen, for otherwise this is all just a showcase. I wonder if there could be a pastoral authority rather than a legal, disciplinary one."

"Well, that is what we would hope for, but can you see all those cardinals, with their medieval faces, agreeing to any change at all?"

"I wonder," thought Miriam, "if it could happen like that time in the British parliament when the House of Lords rejected the proposed bills from the House of Commons, and the Prime Minister, Lloyd George, threatened to create enough new lords to back him and swamp the opposition. Perhaps the Pope could elevate a new set of cardinals."

"Well, we have no choice but to take it very seriously. I'm glad that Niki is there. He turned out to be an excellent negotiator. Can you reach some sort of common mind in our Protestant flock?"

"That's the job for Faith and Order. I'm fortunate that the Moderator for the next three years is Professor Miklos from the Reformed Church in Hungary, and the Vice-Moderator is the Episcopal Bishop of Los Angeles, Veronica Patterson, both very bright people. We'll work hard at it."

How prickly some of these Protestant clerics could be, so reluctant to face radical possibilities. Miriam wrote clear papers with options for the possible discussion, models of realistic thinking, but for some there had only to be a mention of 'bishops' and they turned aside as though threatened with a disease. To Miriam and to most of the members of the Faith and Order Commission it was self-evident that any major reunion of the church would be on the basis of the episcopal ministry, so central was it in the early tradition. What mattered was how that particular ministry was defined and exercised. So a paper on 'Possible Understandings of the Papacy' was regarded as explosive by the Scots and Irish Presbyterians, too hot to handle, and as betrayal by hard-line Calvinists in the United States. Yet it was simple good sense to have thought about this key issue before there was an invitation from Gregory to come together to seek reconciliation.

"1 We may start with history. For 1500 years the papacy was the accepted focus of western Christianity. We were all Catholics then. It is the stem of the vine which grew out of the apostolic root. Of course it was weakened by party politics and family feuds and personal ambitions, but it remained unchallenged as the model for all those centuries. From those centuries have come our Bible and our Psalmody and our faith itself through the missionary activity which popes encouraged. It is worth recalling that the Reformers were urging reform, not division.

2 We all know of the corruptions of power which plagued the papacy, including the infamous Indulgences, the nepotism, the absentee bishops, the contested elections and the persecution of the Inquisition. The Reformers were surely right to reveal these and call for a cleansing of the institution. And it has been dealt with. From the Council of Trent onwards popes have been far more upright in conduct and the whole Catholic Church far more aware of the Holy Spirit's calling and judgement. So in many ways the pleas of the Reformers have been met. But not in all; there are still great matters of the individual approach to God and the institutional authority which are unresolved.

3 We have not yet seen, in Protestantism, any genuine alternative to the papacy as the symbol and focus of the unity of the global church. We have been divided, not only by doctrinal and liturgical matters, but by ethnic and national borders. On occasion we have allowed one powerful voice to lead into schism. We may claim that there is a spiritual unity among us, but the church is a visible presence in the world, and in that respect we are divided. We have no major unity proposal on the table at present.

4 One possible route, therefore, is to recognise the Pope as the Universal Pastor. That would be in line with the commission of Jesus to Peter, "Feed my sheep," and thus with the Rome tradition. In

practice this would mean that the main focus of the Pope's ministry would be to care for the churches where the people are persecuted or oppressed, where they are in danger of forsaking the fellowship, and where disasters bring them great sorrow. It would be a teaching ministry, encouraging faithfulness.

5 A variation would be to regard the Pope as the Global Evangelist, that is, to emphasise the apostolic calling to speak the word of grace, to confront the powers that diminish human life, to encourage those who bring healing and to help the church everywhere to be outward looking. This would be to move the emphasis from all that is internal to the church towards witness at all the frontiers of faith.

6 As the symbol and focus of the unity of Christians, the Pope, as the Bishop of Rome, would preside at international meetings of bishops or Metropolitans. There would need to be a means for appointing an archbishop to deputise, since such gatherings could become frequent. For Protestants this means honouring and welcoming the Pope as their most senior minister. For the Vatican it means living at ease with Reformed devotion and worship.

7 This brings us to the issue of discipline and legal authority. Our plea would be for such matters to be the work of the councils of the church, in whatever pattern is agreeable to the local conditions and the unity of the whole, rather than a personal matter in the hands of the Pope. The pyramid pattern of authority is not essential for the fellowship of Christians, is not fitting for the present age of citizen rights, and invests one person with excessive power. In most of the councils, lay people should be members, particularly when ethical matters are discussed.

8 Since it is plain that all Popes and Councils, Presbyteries and Priests may err, and have erred, we would look for a pattern of regular self-examination and review so that the church is always open to the Holy Spirit and to constant renewal, so that its life may better represent the ministry of the living Christ.

9 These are clearly very considerable reforms which would need great patience in negotiation. It may be that Pope Gregory does not have such radical thoughts in his current plans. This paper is offered

in the hope that the Protestant world communions could be prepared for such a discussion if that opportunity comes."

Well, thought Miriam, that will send a shiver through the ranks, as she sent off copies to the Moderator and Vice-Moderator of the Commission for comment. There will be some who want me sacked and perhaps some who will depart in a huff, but surely we must take some risk if we are ever to do big things for unity. Colleagues in the office felt rejuvenated that at last they were engaged in world-sized issues.

***

7

With its ancient gatehouse, its fine library, and gnarled old fig trees in the grounds, Lambeth Palace hid behind a wall that closed the view of the Thames. Perhaps this was intentional, for the much newer Palace of Westminster across the river had grown in the nineteenth century to be by far the dominant presence. Lambeth and Westminster – the old rival powers of the English state – now shook hands with decorum and protocol. Up the entrance stairs at Lambeth the main public rooms were on the left, to the right were the private office and apartments of the Archbishop of Canterbury, and, inescapable, the portraits of former Archbishops lined almost all the walls, not for their beauty but as a constant reminder of the succession.

The present occupant. John Pearson Donnelly, was a scholar and academic, who had, to the surprise of many, become an excellent pastoral bishop in Manchester. He had been received at Istanbul as a VIP and was impressed with Pope Gregory's approach to the Orthodox. On this June morning he called on the intercom for his ecumenical officer, Max Jolly, to come in and discuss the latest Faith and Order paper from Geneva. He did not know how seriously to take it. Could there truly be an opening for such a discussion?

Max was rather dismissive. "I think it is all a long way off and Dr Menzies is flying a kite, just to see how much backing there would be if the Pope makes an approach to Protestants as he has to the

Orthodox. You talked with the Pope in the Vatican last year, so how do you rate his intentions?"

"I think he must be serious. To have gone this far at Istanbul simply as a publicity exercise is just not his style. He must surely have gauged that there is enough sympathy in the Curia for starting the process. Of course, when the controversial items come up, opposition could force a retreat."

"Well then," Max replied without much conviction, "I think, sir, that it would be useful for you to phone Durham as he is our representative on the Geneva Commission. They are meeting next week."

On the phone the Archbishop asked the Bishop of Durham what he thought of the controversial paper. "It is a preliminary test run. I think Dr Menzies is seeking to discover which of the member communions would be ready to engage in a serious attempt. If the response is entirely negative then we are simply back at the old bilaterals, which have been going on for years without much progress. If we could come together, at the least the five major communions, Anglican, Lutheran, Reformed, Baptist and Methodist, then it would be a new game entirely. I hope we can be positive at that point."

"Yes, I agree. But please don't let people run ahead and assume too much. This is still very preliminary. Somehow Pope Gregory will have to overcome the declaration of Leo XIII that all Anglican ordinations are "utterly invalid and altogether void." That's a pretty big hurdle. So go carefully, Andrew. I'd be glad if you could stop here after the Commission meeting to let me know how things stand."

The Archbishop, feeling that he had enough of the office and the headaches of so many insoluble problems, gladly climbed into the red Austin Mini and drove to King's College in the Strand for a discussion with a lively crowd of students. There he felt at his best, their questioning spirit switching on his own probing mind. Why does faith matter? Can't we lead good lives without faith? Why do you speak of God as having the character of a man? Do you really think that God interferes with our lives? He had no simple answers but was skilled in leading the students to think more deeply about questions which had faced the church for two millennia. He knew that repeating old answers was useless in a world where the very concept of the divine was washed out of the European psyche, so it was good to start with the wonder of life in all its complexity. 'Start where people are' was the motto of evangelists from the time when Paul preached at Athens and it still held good.

***

A press statement which appeared in Pravda reported briefly, "Owing to a medical condition, President Yumin has resigned and is receiving specialist treatment. The Russian people will be grateful for the long service that Comrade Yumin has given to the nation and will wish him well. The Central Committee has appointed Comrade Igor Rubetsky to assume the Presidency."

And Comrade Rubetsky was enjoying his grand new office, the uniformed attendants and clerks, the security men who were suddenly his loyal servants, and his access to all the intelligence files, with endless entertaining details of the follies of the great. He was not enjoying the reports that reached his desk every day about civil unrest verging on open rebellion. From the Caucasus region the inspiration seemed to be an Islamic nationalism, with intense local rivalries which grew from ancient feuds. In Eastern Europe the grip of the USSR was resented and now was fuelled by the Catholic opposition to atheistic Communism. It was a thorny bundle. Whatever forces the military might throw at disturbances, bloody wounds would result. Rubetsky did not want his name to become a second Stalin, but neither could he afford weakness that might lead to the collapse of the Union. The whole world knew that the Union was welded together by bullets and blood. Could it be maintained only in that same way? He addressed his inner circle of ministers.

"You probably think in the old terms of throwing the weight of the army at these disturbances in the Caucasus, but I am going to be a little more careful, for I don't want the whole of the western world on our necks for brutality and opposing freedom – that has done us no good in the past. So I am going for a little finesse.

You will follow these instructions. Select three or four of the leaders in each of those language groups. Bring them into the local police headquarters. Treat them well. Tell them they must stop entirely their political activities. Send them home. See what they do. If they persist, bring them in with their families. Tell them that as they have not learnt the lesson, consequences follow. Keep one child in detention, treated well. Send the family home. See what they do. If they still persist then you can begin serious harassment. A fire which destroys the home can be very unsettling. But, you see, start gently, give them a chance to reform. I think that will be excellent propaganda. The army goes in as a last resort. We don't want another Afghanistan, so just a little finesse.

In Hungary, Czechoslovakia and Poland it is a very different story, for they have never been part of our Union and so feel alienated, and now the churches there are becoming the focus of dissent. We have to treat all that with patience. If the people want to be Catholics, then we don't really care. But if the churches are used for politics, then we shut them down. I hear that in East Germany the Protestant churches are full of young people praying for the downfall of communism. Well, let them pray. But if they start marching or broadcasting, shut them down. We must draw a clear line. Tell the bishops, Stick to your prayers, that's your job.

Is all that quite clear?"

"Yes, sir. We will inform the departmental heads."

"Now here in Moscow we have always had a careful watch on the priests and I can assure you this will continue. I have just had word that Patriarch Olav is retiring from office; he's a bit senile. So we will see who is nominated to follow him. I will deal personally with that."

He looked around the circle, hoping for full approval but the faces revealed little. They were ready to give him his chance at shaping policy but leadership was now such an uncertain business, so unsteady, that bureaucrats needed to plan exit routes and safe deposit boxes. Rubetsky had no great guiding passion or philosophy, he was a pragmatist and his intention was to hold things together while the economy evolved towards private ownership and initiative. It was an uncomfortable ride. For some of the old guard it was communism betrayed; for the younger generation it was too slow and too piecemeal a reform to satisfy; for bankers and industrialists it looked like a heavy door that needed just a push to open the way to wealth.

It was in June, when the whole of Russia was bursting with the flowers of summer, a revelation in green leaf, scarlet geranium, purple iris, girls in sundresses, dachas reopened and potato plots weeded, that Rubetsky learned that the new Patriarch had been appointed. He was Boris Minchov, a sixty year old from the Urals, well thought of as a wise pastor, a writer of thoughtful essays and a lover of the Russian language and literature.

Invited to the Kremlin for a lunch with Rubetsky, the new Patriarch found that it was a private meeting, restrained with the formalities of 'Mr President' and 'Your Grace'.

"You are to be congratulated, Your Grace, and you will have our respect as a leader of the faithful. You know, and I know, that the history of our beloved nation and the history of the Orthodox Church are bound up together. I will not interfere with your spiritual duties."

"I appreciate that, Mr President, for there is a great deal to do if we are to hold the loyalty of the younger generation for the faith. You will know from my record that I have never been a great friend to communism or the Party, but that is something you understand is endemic to the clergy, so we will surely respect each other."

"Yes, indeed. But I suggest that you be careful."

Minchov looked at him straight in the eye, "Could you please be explicit. We need to know the basis for our relationship."

"I cannot have the Church exploiting anti-Moscow agitation. I know that you would never suggest such folly, but there are people who are tempted that way. They get their inspiration from the Catholics in Europe. There they are turning the faith into a political campaign. They speak about freedom from the chains of the Party. About the evils of atheism and the work of Lenin. About a different regime, a new government. Now all that is politics, and it is not the business of the clergy. Do you understand me?"

"Thank you, that is very clear. But you will also need to know that as a priest in the household of God, I am not going to become your active promoter or advocate or party man, for that too is entering your political field. I will try to serve the Church. I will give all I have to serve our people. But I will keep an independent mind and not give myself to other ties and loyalties."

"This is a good start, for now we both know to be careful. Let us continue to be frank with each other."

"Thank you, Mr President. I am sure you know that everywhere the Church in its liturgy will be praying for you. I wish you well. And thanks for this very good spring lamb."

It is Watch Your Step, Minchov thought, as the Kremlin driver silently steered the limousine to take him home. But the Patriarch had a weapon in his armoury which he hoped would never be needed. It dated back to 1944 when he was a newly ordained priest in a war damaged rural area not very far from the bitter fighting. One month the locals had been surprised to find that military trucks were depositing crates to the property of the local party boss, where they were shielded from the weather under tarpaulins. They turned out to be full of army supplies, boots, greatcoats, trousers, belts, shirts, warm socks, metal plates and mugs. all very easy to sell on the black market. The party boss did very well indeed. Where had it all come from? Minchov had been told by the wide-awake teenagers that the markings on the trucks pointed to a brigade stationed on the front not far away. The infantry there were desperately short of supplies and the officer responsible for the stores was a Major Rubetsky. A young priest could do nothing about such military matters, but it stayed in his mind as one of the criminal acts which are shuffled under the carpet during the chaos of a great war. Now, at last, he thought, it is indeed time for Mr President to be careful.

***

Little Katrina was enjoying the Crimea summer, crawling out to the grass behind the house where Petrovna had a comfortable chair. Swallows raised their brood in nests under the eaves. A large-bosomed neighbour, wearing her swimsuit, was watering her vegetable patch. The cancer treatment was exhausting. Petrovna was still losing weight. Niki was tender in his care for her, thoughtful, doing the chores, but this week was away for a meeting of the Reconciliation Council in Athens. There the meeting was guided by Cardinal Terracini to work steadily through the list of outstanding issues, to see what might be approached most readily, for his correspondence with Olav had shown that if a minor matter could be resolved then it was encouragement to tackle the major blockages. And encouragement was needed. Both teams had a good mixture of the learned, the eager, the wise and the narrow-minded. Both had to struggle to break the chains of history.

The Cardinal was at his most diplomatic. "We have been given a great task, an exciting hope, with no guarantee of success at the end. We will all agree with the objective, to cancel all the old edicts which affirmed the separation and so bring into being a new reconciled communion. But we will inevitably disagree on some of the steps that will have to be taken if we are to reach that end.

So this is a risky business. It is plain that if we push too hard and with too radical proposals, then large portions of our faithful people will reject our work. For there are many who understand their faith as the continuous repetition of what has always been done – and that is not such a bad definition of religion for people with simple minds. So I would urge that we seek to shape our proposals as the natural development of trends that already are with us. We don't have to break the churches apart in order to bring them together.

But confession is surely part of the process, as it always must be for Christians, and I am prepared to share our confession with you – not for the minutes, please, but to listen to the Spirit.

In the western church, the Roman church, the church which we call Catholic, we have, through the centuries, emphasised too heavily the territorial, political and legal power of the hierarchy rather than the humble service and pastoral caring which Christ gives us as the model of ministry. It is as though the mantle of the emperors slipped onto the shoulders of the popes. The worldly power led to corruption in many forms, including superstition, to neglect of serious biblical study and to the domination of the laity by the clergy. That we confess. We have learnt that we have to take another road so that the power is always the power of the Holy Spirit and not of the imperium, the triple crown. That stays, where it should, in the museum of history.

We confess that too often the Church became the ally of despots, and neglected the persecuted. Indeed it became a persecutor itself through all the years of the Inquisition. The Church, led by the hierarchy, abused the Jews and so helped to lay some of the foundations for the most terrible holocaust of our era. We were late and timid in the fight against the slave trade.

We confess that we misunderstood the wonder of science, the marvellous advances of the human mind in understanding the universe. We were too protective of the old world of clerical dominance, perhaps too afraid of human ability to fashion new communities and fight the plagues. We were – and perhaps still are – unable to appreciate the revolution in the position of women. I hope that you have seen signs that we are catching up, but this is a confession of our past failures.

Now I have been very open to you. The Catholic Church has indeed been facing the need for reform in many ways for many years; we are slow and cautious; we are learners. But that is the way in which we will seek to deal with change, in order that the whole body of the faithful might travel with us."

A respectful silence. Then Archbishop Stanislav of Kiev, who led the Othordox team, felt bound to respond.

"In gratitude for such openness, we also know that there is much to confess. It is not an easy thing to do, for we are much more accustomed to praising the Lord for so many blessings rather than facing our weaknesses.

But now let us confess that the Orthodox have been, and still are, so wedded to our ethnic and national groups that church and state live like a married couple. This has meant that the church has been unable to raise any effective opposition to the cruelties of the state. Indeed we have, in many cases, just kept silent. We have always backed the state in war. We have made friends with despots. This has led us to embracing racism too often. So although many priests have been eager to serve the oppressed, the public face of the church has been closed to them.

Then I believe that we ought to confess – and here my colleagues might not agree with me – that we enjoyed for too long the pattern of aristocracy on top and the peasantry down below. It was all so convenient. It helped to preserve the church. The aristocrats could finance us, the peasants could believe us. Duty prevailed. We were too slow to see that the movements towards education and industry and the new middle class were revolutionary and called for a new pattern of local church life.

Alongside that I would put our suspicion of all other churches, yes, our distrust of the Catholics. We have tended to preserve our territory so strongly, to hold that national character so tightly, that any other variety of Christian discipleship appeared an invader. So where the Orthodox world and the Catholic world meet, we have seen misunderstandings, squabbles and sporadic violence. We have failed to love our sisters and brothers in the faith.

From this confession we would make a new beginning. You have indicated, dear Cardinal, that the Catholic Church moves slowly. I assure you it is a sprinter compared with the Orthodox. We shall need a sharp spur if this Reconciliation Council is to achieve what the Pope asked at Istanbul. So we pray that the Spirit may move us to be more generous and more courageous than in the past. That is how we would work together."

It was a promising start. Confession is not only good for the soul, it is good for human relations. So as they listed the issues which had caused and then maintained the separation of the churches, planned their future meetings and their secretariat, Niki felt hopeful that there would be some real progress. It was not so simple to keep a hopeful spirit back home, for the cancer treatment was proving physically draining. Petrovna was determined to be a good patient and together they were cheerfully optimistic about the outcome, but inwardly, at night, fear chilled the brave hopes. Katrina was a blessing, growing, energetic, healthy, sometimes comical, always ready for a cuddle, the very image of life.

They discussed whether Petrovna's mother might come south for the period of the treatment. She was now 70, on her own, and determined to keep her Moscow flat. The housing shortage was acute, and any empty flat might well be either broken into by squatters or taken over by the city authorities. So she wanted to remain in situ. Also she was an awkward person, becoming more acidic as she became older, sharp in her comments and judgements, not given to everyday chatter, her eyes wary and her manner abrupt. Niki was uncomfortable with her, a little scared, so could not press her sincerely to come to Crimea and live with them. Petrovna was wise enough to appreciate this, for she too found that her mother had become a chilly presence rather than the embracing carer of her childhood. Most mothers have a late blooming as grandmothers, but a few become too fearful of age to forget their frailty and so to rejoice in new life.

***

In Moscow heavy thunder clouds and torrents of rain marked the end of August, the streets awash and Red Square a desolate scene. There was a public sense of unease; old certainties were shaken by the spread of information, reports by travellers and the news of violent clashes in the Caucasus. The propaganda about the West was still the same – "acute industrial slavery, millionaires and grinding poverty, war lords and armament manufacturers, lying politicians" and so on, but the realities were slowly getting through. The rapid change in leadership quickened this sense of uncertainty. Some Western correspondents were even talking about a pre-1917 mood, but the times were quite dissimilar. Then the disturbances were heading somewhere, some objective, however vague, was there in the smoke, a new dawn. Now, in the late 70's, there was no direction, just this discomfort of knowing that the old ways of absolute Party control were breaking down and that the boundaries of the empire were no longer sacred.

President Rubetsky was aware but wholly unable to understand, for he had no philosophy of politics behind him, only the pragmatism of the old soldier buffeted by the storm of economics and general distrust. His base in the Party was uninsured. The Patriarch Minchov was on the upswing of the pendulum, for he was a far more acute thinker, could see the weakening of the Party hegemony, and believed that the Church would benefit, not only in Eastern Europe but throughout Russia. "I don't need to threaten," he thought, "for he is a weak character and will be folded away by the new populists like cardboard in a rubbish bin."

But the Russian empire was vast and well-engineered, from Berlin to Vladivostok, the satrapies of Eastern Europe being the weakest element, regarded in Moscow as the fruits of a war which was beginning to fade from the popular memory. Yes, they had communist governments and a Russian military presence, the police information service was thorough, but somehow the Poles, Czechs, Hungarians, and Germans managed to flaunt an independent spirit and treat the Russians as unwelcome visitors. Liberators had become guards.

It was all very puzzling as Rubetsky, in his Kremlin office, heard the thunder rattling the ancient domes of the Treasury. His first concern was always the army. Although his war had been as a transport and supply officer, he knew the system and remembered the heroes. When they paraded through Red Square he brought out the medals and clapped with pride, but he also knew that the officers were mostly near retirement, had static minds, and had to make do with much out of date weaponry. The popular mood was all against enlistment. Stories of recruits being worked to death, tested beyond capability, sexually abused, and starved of rations were featured in illegal, duplicated leaflets. In fact the whole military-industrial complex was so corrupt that only constant favours could produce the equipment needed, and Rubetsky was not the man to scrub the dirt.

His relief came in the shape of Lieutenant Vransky, a personal aide, athletic, blonde, agile, always available to slide out of her uniform as readily as smooth, shining chestnuts dropped their spiky shells. His adventure was to travel to New York for the General Assembly of the United Nations with four security men, two secretaries, two Central Committee colleagues, a military communications expert, a doctor, a speech writer and Vransky to take care of personal needs. The ambassador had booked the top floor of the hotel, which soon became a little Russia, the great vases of chrysanthemums and dahlias luminous against the dark curtains, luxury hidden behind the muscle men, chilled vodka on tap.

The speech began with a reference to American history. "We honour the memory of the revolution, yes, the American revolution, which resisted the oppressive policy of Britain and set this nation on the path to independence. It is a fine story of courage. We, too, have our revolution. We honour those who died in order to set us on the road towards a new society, freed from the grip of a feudal aristocracy. We are still building this nation of citizens. Four million of our people died in the Great Patriotic War to defend it. And we will defend it, make no mistake about that.

"The principle which guides us here in this Assembly is that we are not to interfere with the internal life of any other nation, for every nation has its right to live its own life according to its culture and philosophy. (A voice from the back of the hall, Ask the Hungarians.) We will not allow any other nation to create unrest in the Soviet Union. We will identify any who undermine our economy, and any who broadcast lies about us. We know how to defend ourselves. It is a sad fact that this nation, this America, is the source of the most pernicious propaganda, building its military forces to threaten us and pretending that its capitalist system is triumphant.

"That is a Hollywood fiction. We represent the new society. We inspire the peoples of Africa and Asia with hope for radical change. Socialism means justice and care for all. Capitalism is doomed as the few at the top crow about their wealth and force the masses to work for low wages. Capitalism is just the re-invention of the feudal system translated into economics. It cannot be sustained. It will die of inequality and injustice.

All politics is about power. Governments can use their power to support the wealthy or to bring justice for all. Russia is a great nation, pledged to build the human society where everyone is cared for and everyone contributes, the society where everyone supports the national vision. The vast distances across our land and the variety of languages and cultures are all bound into one love of the motherland, making us a strong voice here among the nations."

And so on. The speechwriter may have believed it, but Rubetsky knew that Russia was also a house of cards, stuck together by corruption, lagging far behind in modernisation, with a hundred million poor people who struggled to get one decent meal a day. They could launch rockets to outer space but not get fresh vegetables to market. Somehow, through all those Stalin years, the priorities had become twisted so that military power always came first, and hungry bellies did not count at all. Rubetsky did not know what he could possibly do about it. In New York he looked around at prosperity, travelled in comfort and bought luxuries at the glamorous stores. Could the old bombast be sustained? He had too many doubts to be a convincing waver of the red flag.

Back at the hotel, he looked forward to relaxation with Vransky, so skilled in invigorating a man of mature years. She was not readily available.

"Where is Vransky?" he demanded of the security men.

"She went down to get some pastries at the snack bar, sir."

"Did you sit here and not go with her? What were you doing?"

"Sir, you took two of us, with the doctor and the speech writer with you to the UN building for your personal security there. We were left here to ensure the security of the communications equipment."

"How long has she been gone?"

"It's about 40 minutes, sir."

"Then get down there and find the girl, you fools."

But she was not found. She had disappeared into the New York crowds and might end up anywhere. Rubetsky was furious, not so much by the personal loss but because if the girl had defected and this were to be published then he would appear a pathetic loser, not the Presidential figure of a great nation. It could hardly have turned out worse, for she had approached a couple of police on duty, told them she was seeking asylum and as a personal aide of the President could be very useful to the American government, was taken to police headquarters, interviewed at length, charmed everyone, was taken by car to a safe house with a policewoman as housemate, and then, next day, taken to a TV studio for a late evening chat show. There were heavy jokes about an "aide de camp." The Russian delegation made immediate arrangements for a flight home.

Back in Moscow the four security men were immediately arrested at the airport, stripped of all privileges and reassigned to

Yakutsk on the Lena river in Siberia to work with the labour gangs on roadbuilding. The President, knowing that he had been made to look foolish, aired his frustration by ordering a more aggressive policy towards all those rebellious spirits who were stirring trouble on the periphery of the Soviet Union. He felt aggrieved, isolated and betrayed, and so became more dangerous by the day.

***

In Geneva the autumn was golden, the vine leaves, birch and beech trees, chrysanthemums, pumpkins and chillies, long dry grasses, and the late sloping sunshine all gilding the lakeside. In the World Council offices, Miriam Menzies was busy shepherding her rather unruly flock of denominations towards a common process for responding to the Vatican. She also was concerned for Niki and Petrovna, for there had been letters in which Niki had shared his deep worry about the illness. She wondered whether the hospital in the Crimea had the latest technology and the most effective drugs, especially when compared with the advanced cancer centres in Switzerland. But the very thought of moving such a patient, husband and little child would be costly and might lead to nothing, and Niki could hardly maintain his important work away from his office.

It was one of those pastoral problems which has no simple answer, perhaps no answer at all except prayer, hope and love. The activism of the Protestant tradition presses the conscience to be up and doing, to fight the evil, to expel the darkness, to launch a programme, but there is also a call, at some times of distress, to acknowledge our powerlessness, to be quiet and keep that candle alight in the heart. The religious communities of the Catholic tradition, now so much reduced, may yet have great themes and disciplines to share.

Through the autumn, Miriam's main work was the preparation of the meeting of the Faith and Order Division. which would be held in Madras in January. Relations with the Vatican were one major item, but there were others equally testing. How should the mainline denominations react to the Pentecostal movement with the growth of independent, enthusiastic, congregations which had no regular ministry but great delight in the signs of spiritual power? Their reading of the Bible seemed uneducated, their worship was irregular but they had something that the older bodies lacked, revolutionary change in people's lives. There were other sorts of independence. In Africa particularly congregations were growing rapidly around individual cult figures, some of them claiming healing miracles, others oracles of wisdom, abounding in colourful uniforms, all raising large sums in collections. Some preachers were seen driving luxury cars. How should they be understood – part of the world church of Christ or false prophets? Another major project was to write a liturgy for the Eucharist which would be agreeable to all the major denominations and could become a symbol of their unity, a test indeed of how theology and poetry and history might flow into accessible language and action.

In Madras the meetings were held in a Lutheran college property. Crisp mornings, heat at noon, gay shamianas, devoted cooks, stray monkeys, taciturn Ethiopians, argumentative Americans, superior Anglicans, humble cleaners, unlimited cups of tea and thoughtful worship in the college chapel all brought the campus alight. Miriam stressed in her introduction that they were gathered to do positive work for unity and not the negative business of criticism and complaint, "What we have to share by the grace of God is to be placed on the table for all."

But it soon became clear that there were those present whose main aim was to condemn Miriam for her adventurous papers. Among these the Irish Presbyterians were the most vocal, people whose defensive position in Northern Ireland made them prickly and emotional. "You think there are positive aspects of the papacy which we might accept. Never, never, never. Our people believe that the papacy was a wrong turning by the early church, was corrupted beyond salvation and places a fallible man in an impossible position which has nothing to do with the mercy of Christ." They had clearly come prepared for a boycott of the proceedings.

Sleepless in her strange bed, Miriam wondered whether she had been too radical. Was there to be no other way to find unity but to lose friends? Was divisiveness so written into the Protestant psyche that every new adventure meant a new fracture in fellowship? If so, was the status quo sacred? It could not be. After the journey of a hundred years there could be no full stop to ecumenism, the only way was forward to greater integration or understanding. But no new birth without pain.

How strange it is, she thought, that some of us are gripped by history so tightly that any reform is rejected even before it has been considered. The walls may be crumbling and the barbarians at the gate but some will still trust in the sacrifice at the temple to save them. The Mongol army may be breaching the Great Wall but the worship of ancestors must be observed. So the popes may have changed out of all recognition since the corruptions of the dark ages, but still, in the darker corners of Protestantism, they are derided as the scarlet woman of Revelations. Part myth, part ignorance, part rhetoric, yet such popular appeal, there is the blockage to reform.

At this first look at the Catholic/Reformed relationship by the Commission, the majority of the members were ready to take a thoughtful step forward. "Will you, won't you, will you, won't you will you join the dance?" The naysayers appeared as intellectual lightweights when they stood aside at morning coffee, but they represented their constituency, that uncritical mass of church people, familiar with poverty – perhaps in the southern states of the US – and grateful to the old church which had given them confidence to deal with disadvantage.

When Miriam flew back after the meeting she had secured approval to write to Cardinal Terracini to say that there would be a unified attempt to respond if the Vatican should come forward with a serious quest for a path to reconciliation. Perhaps, on the world scale of achievements, this was very minor, a mere scratch of the pen, but for those involved, the leaders of the distinct traditions, it was a leap of faith. As soon as she was back in Geneva, Miriam was invited to dinner by Walter Schwartz and Lucy to give them a first-hand account of the Madras meeting.

"My own lot, the Church of Scotland, found it difficult. You know how frightened the Scots are of bishops, and any move in that direction raises the temper of debate. But they came along. The

Anglicans were enthusiastic at this preliminary stage. Good support from the United churches in India. But I'm afraid we have lost the Irish Presbyterians and the Southern Baptists."

"Do you think", asked Walter, "that they could stay with us in the other Divisions of the Council and just resign from the Faith and Order Commission?"

"I can't say. There was some pretty angry comment in the corridor."

"It's remarkable"' Lucy said, "that this is stirring us up just at the time when the European Community is dealing with the British. Are they truly in or just sitting on the edge? Can they have the benefits without the burdens? Such a foolish ambivalence it seems to us in Germany."

"Well", said Miriam, "we have always been on the edge. That's being an island. But we can be pretty bloody minded too. It's as though nationalism beats rational thought every time. But it's also that we were not part of the Nazi empire, not a conquered people, so have not faced the same pressures of renewal."

"So let us have another glass and drink to hope", Walter was not going to allow the difficulties to cloud the evening and the work ahead.

***

In Rome Cardinal Terracini and Pope Gregory were having a similar conversation.

"Holy Father, I am now able to report on the first two meetings of the full Reconciliation Council. They have gone remarkably well as we have tried to sketch the programme ahead. One of the first items was to define the objective, and perhaps I may read you the minute which we agreed.

'We seek to enable the two communions to accept each other as equal sharers in the grace of Christ and equal partners in the service of Christ, with full recognition of ordained ministries, and full hospitality at the Holy Table. We seek to be at one in theological endeavour and biblical study, to resolve all disputes as members of one family and to give equal honour to both traditions. We seek a resolution to the issue of authority by limiting the judicial functions of hierarchy and stressing the pastoral calling to support the weak and to proclaim the presence of the Kingdom of the risen Christ.'

That took a bit of time to set down, as you can imagine. But it gives us a target for the next series of meetings."

"Thank you, my brother. If you can come anywhere close to that aim then you will be doing something like a miracle. We can have no illusions about the difficulty."

"That is something I have learnt. Several of our colleagues here have warned me that there will be steady opposition. Particularly strong words have come from the Cardinals from Mexico, Poland and Nigeria – a strange mix – especially as they have little experience of the Orthodox in their countries. Those close to the frontier, in the Balkans, and those close to the Orthodox diaspora, are the most supportive. Perhaps, Father, you might be able to say a word about the ministry of reconciliation when the opportunity comes."

"Of course that's possible. Such opposition means that you will need to have each step of your progress well-argued and shown to be both practical and well-founded. But now you also have word, I think, from the Protestant world."

"Yes, the matter has been taken up very seriously through the World Council of Churches, and several of the larger groups, the Anglicans, Methodists, Presbyterians and Reformed, and the Lutherans, have all agreed that if we wish to move into a process, then they will meet us together rather than one by one. This is their attempt to move things rather more quickly than through those bilateral dialogues which seem to have taken generations."

"We will surely take up that response. But I think, my brother, that you will have enough on your plate with the Orthodox, so I want to appoint another Cardinal to head the discussions with the children of the Reformation. My choice is Timothy Donald at Westminster. He is close to the Protestants in Britain and since the Anglicans are a key part of this discussion, to have the Cardinal and the Archbishop both in the same place should help the conversation."

"I am grateful, Father, for such good help. And I think we should also have a fresh secretary at that table. Or else we shall become too congested in the office. Perhaps someone from the Americas who is working here. There's a Father O'Keefe in Evangelisation who is said to be a wizard at office organisation; he's from Boston."

"Give that a try. See if you can gather the two teams together, say, six months from now. My timetable is crowded – there's a visit to South Africa next month - and I would wish to be there for the opening meeting. There will be plenty of work to tackle before the meeting, on both sides. My secretary will call Timothy Donald today and say that I wish him to come for a discussion about the route ahead."

***

It was domestic matters which concerned Niki and Petrovna and had pushed the high church agenda into second place, for the illness was taking a firm hold. It was not that pain was invading Petrovna's life with insistent power, but weakness which made even the simpler domestic tasks almost impossible. There were days when she could no longer lift Katrina from her bed for a cuddle. The weight loss was plain. The worry, the fear, were never far away.

Semfiropol seemed to be a city with an unlimited supply of amateur physicians. They gave out pamphlets outside the hospital, bustling, chatty, convinced that the cure was there in the boiled leaves of this marsh plant or that bulb, or in a new diet of fish and dried fruit, or in drinking ten glasses of peppermint tea every day. Should they try everything? Do you clutch at straws? Niki talked with Bishop Konstantin and Mrs Rubetz, who were full of practical good sense but who shook their heads at the barrage of cures.

"If they were genuine," said the bishop, "then they would be universally popular, but in fact these cures lead to more disillusion. It's up to you both. I don't think such cures will turn the tide but then they probably won't do much harm either."

"Do you think the hospital here is as good as we can get?"

"Well, it's not up to the latest New York clinic, of course not, but it has doctors with long experience. You should just ask if they want to refer Petrovna elsewhere. But please feel free to bring Katrina here when you need to be in the office and we will make sure she is well cared for."

"That's a blessing. But, bishop, I am afraid."

"That's just our humanity, my son, for to see your loved one declining in such a way, gradually losing the strength of life – that is one of the most distressing things we have to face. Easier, I guess, to face the bullets in war, the sudden shock. But we are within the church and surrounded by prayer, so our fear blends with the confidence that God's presence is still with us even in the valley of the shadow, for it is the presence of light. I preach that often enough for I believe it is the basic truth of life. Let that confidence keep you on track, Nicholas. Now, as a very practical matter, how do you think Petrovna would react if I can find one of our nursing sisters to come to you every morning to see to Petrovna's toilet and breakfast, and do Katrina's washing and her food for the day?"

"I think that would be wonderful. Please go ahead, Bishop."

EMPIRE CRUMBLE

A carelessness reigned in those days of crumbling empires. Senators spoke but nobody listened. Chiefs raised a tribal flag, crowds followed, greed prevailed and the storehouses were ransacked, spilling grain and blood. From Babylon to Rome to Spain to the Ottomans it was always a bitter process, an erosion of confidence. Soldiers deserted and slaves revolted. Life may have been no better than before, the old authority gone, but some would claim "At last we are free."

So we saw the French admit that the hour had come, the terrors in Algeria should end, and the colonists, resentful, pack up. Then the British, gentlemen of standing and intellect, were bankrupt. India gone in a fury of slash, burn and kill. The flag lowered at midnight, a new flag raised. New rulers, raised on rhetoric, across Africa. It's the old empire crumble.

Now it's Russia's turn. Berlin to Vladivostok, the Barents Sea to the Oxus, a great congregation of traditions, cultures, languages, politics, religions, held together by mutual suspicion, armoured divisions, secret police and multiple gaols. But now without driving passion or conviction. Building space rockets – a diversion. So the map begins to tear at the edges and for every head chopped off, a dozen seem to appear. The realists say, Let them go.

Who is next? Why, it must be America, the super power. Almighty dollar tumbles and banks close their doors. Use the army and then find that the chaos left behind is worse than the devil you fought.

Have we woken up from imperial dreaming? Has the magisterium disrobed? Is it cultivate your garden and forget the Wild Wood? Am I my brother's keeper? Still I hear the old voice calling, "There is only one family of humanity", and a new voice sings, "This is the day of the little people and no emperor can imprison our hope or command our assent."

I wonder, can they hear that voice in Washington and Beijing and Moscow? No empire lasts for ever. But is the instinct for dominance, under the name of security, everlasting? The question is clear, but not the answer. Perhaps we could ask Phillip II in the Escorial or Louis XIV at Versailles or Stalin in Red Square, or, how mundane, Benjamin Disraeli picking primroses for Queen Victoria.

8

Within six months Petrovna was failing fast. Overcome with the loss of weight and weakness, she spent time in hospital where the attention was competent, the living rough and the treatment ineffective. It was the next spring when she died, quietly and unprotesting, too drowsy to say farewell. No-one could say it was unexpected, but for Niki it was still the greatest intimate blow of his life. He realised that it was the experience of millions. It was common to human life. But no, it was unique. The great gap had its own shape which he alone could know. This loving, effective, gracious, cheerful presence which had been his delight from the first days of his engagement to her, this lover who knew him through and through, and now this mother who had cherished the most lively daughter, all gone. Gone to glory? He had faith but somehow this did not comfort him, while the absence chilled him.

Bishop Konstantin, with much practical good sense, assured Niki that they would make his office workable and would ease the strain of domestic life with Katrina. He urged Niki to continue with the major task of the Reconciliation Council, and Archbishop Stanislav phoned from Kiev with condolences and hopes that he would stay at his post. From Geneva, kind and thoughtful letters came from Walter Schwartz and Marion Menzies and even one from Elspeth Beach, who had been such a disturbing fan in that office. Messages came from the members of the Joint Committee and the Moscow

Patriarchate, and from Cardinal Terracini in Rome. It was as though the church, in its many faces, was gathering around him so that he would not be alone in his mourning.

Work consumed him. Encouraging all the members of the Orthodox team, he soon found that the Serbian Orthodox were the laggards, still entangled in prejudice, the Greeks were the most fussy, needing every word examined for a whole morning session, and the Russians the most confident, and so the most ready to consider something new. Increasingly impatient with the more trivial issues, and perhaps influenced by Miriam in Geneva, Niki was eager to set the Reconciliation Council to work on the basic matters. He understood the history to show that the struggle between the eastern and western church was not, at its root, about theology or worship but about power. Here were two centres of power, Rome and Constantinople; it was spiritual power and also financial and political to some degree. Neither could bear to be other than in control.

How far that seemed from the message of the New Testament. It sounded more like Caiaphas and Pilate. Where were the humility, the cross-bearing, the foot washing, the healing spirit? So Niki realised that any repetition of the old quarrel would be a false trail. They would have to seek a fresh sort of headship. That was something worth doing, not ecclesiastical fuss about trivia, and if that was in the mind of pope and patriarch then it would be a public witness to the origin of faith. But there were days when the papers on his desk were particularly boring or when a Bulgarian or a Ukrainian bishop wrote in the old defensive mode, so that he wanted to walk away and leave them to it. His particular path of service had made him a reformer, but how could others – isolated, bound tight into routine – reach the same conclusions.

In the evenings Niki wrote Thank You letters to all those who had sent their condolences. When he came to Elspeth Beach, his mind wandered, he thought of her admiration and her youth. He could not erase some erotic dreams flitting through his mind. So his letter was deliberately ambiguous. "Perhaps the work we are both doing will enable us to meet again, and I look forward to that." No, that was too pushy, made him out as too eager. "It was a pleasure to work with you in Faith and Order and I appreciate your friendship." A pleasure? It had been very embarrassing. But why not say it? Here am I, now thirty nine, a celibate life for the last six months, and I'm not a monk. Let's see what happens.

The response came by return. She was thinking of taking some leave to travel and had connections in the city of Odessa, where her father, as a young man, had been involved in a shipping company. Perhaps she could include the Crimea for a day or two. It was her big Russia adventure, once in a lifetime. "Yes", he replied," just tell me your dates when you have your tickets and your visa and I will see where best to contact you. I will look forward to introducing you to Katrina." There, that is a little safety note; it's not just you and me.

Two months later Niki was at the local airport. Elspeth came into the arrivals area, wearing light grey slacks and a black, fluffy jumper, with a rainproof jacket, and carrying a large backpack. Her smile was young and eager. She was full of her impressions of Odessa, what a great city, and, yes, I found the building where the old shipping company had been – of course it's all different now – and they showed me the old brass plate that used to be on the door. Now, to see you is such a relief because you know my Geneva life and we can talk. I bring you good wishes from Miriam, who is still doing a great job. So the chatter went on while they drove to the office, where Elspeth was introduced to Timoteo Tachek, the clerk, and Mrs Rubetz, who was looking after Katrina. Timoteo was busy arranging the travel and accommodation for the next meeting of the Orthodox in the Reconciliation Council, which was to be held in Kiev. Niki explained that Elspeth was doing the same sort of work in Geneva with the Protestants, so they could exchange ideas. But as they drove off they left behind some raised eyebrows and suspicious thoughts about so young a consultant.

The drive home was quick, the chatter easy and Katrina was busy with a string of big coloured beads. It was not until the evening, when Elspeth was going to the hotel she had booked in the town, that things became… embarrassing…exciting? The house was quiet. She asked to go to the bathroom. Then she appeared, wearing only her rainproof jacket and white bikini pants, as odd a bundle of erotic romance as Niki could ever have imagined. Could he walk away, or shoo her back to the bathroom? Such a young admirer, ready and willing, was a powerful sensation, and Niki had been alone long enough to be utterly captivated by the possibility of a playmate in bed.

Any hesitations flitted through his mind at subliminal speed and were dismissed. He embraced her with enthusiasm, ran up the stairs with her to the bedroom, flicking off the lights on the way. Then kissed her, long and deeply, took off her jacket and pushed her, not very gently, onto the bed. He scrambled to take off his clothes and joined her, stroking and kissing as though at his first meal after a fast. Elspeth was not at all dismayed. She was not inexperienced, for her years at college had been educative in many ways. "I've no condoms." "Don't worry, I'm on the pill." So she responded with growing excitement, admiring Niki's strong body. But then, at the critical moment, failure. Niki could not perform, flaccid as an old piece of cord. He rolled aside, angry with himself, and his mood of frustration and shame cooled the temperature. "Don't worry. It will come right later."

But no, it was not to be. He knew the trouble. They were in Petrovna's bed. They were her sheets, given to them by her mother. Her familiar scent was there. She was cuddling Katrina there. She was loving him there. And her picture was on the screen of his mind. The mistake had been to attempt this at home. Perhaps somewhere else, in a new context, an anonymous bed, a fresh discovery, it would come right. But is that what he truly wanted? He had seen a playmate, but Elspeth had hoped for a partner. All his training stirred the moral confusion in his mind. Should he let her lead him on? Or where should he lead? Desirable, yes indeed, for she had a quick intelligence, common interests and vigorous, healthy sexuality. But to be serious too soon might open the way to future tragedy, for they came from such different cultures; he could never be English, but neither could Elspeth become a Russian of the decaying Soviet Union with the burden of blood and poverty heavy in the soul.

So he temporised. Waking early, he made a pot of tea and took a cup to the bedroom for Elspeth. "Today is Sunday and I'm not expected anywhere, so why not take a trip to Yalta and let Katrina have a paddle, and then, if we feel like it, we could stay there overnight and drive back early tomorrow so that I can go to work and you can make your connection at the airport?"

"Yes, yes, that would be splendid, to see that famous coast."

"But can we do this as close, dear friends, without assuming we belong to each other for ever?"

"Yes, Niki, I understand. But I want to be with you and love you more than anything else in my life and I can't wash that away. I'll try to keep it under wraps. I won't pester you."

"I know you care so much, but I just need a bit more time to recover – the loss has been a great thing in my life. But let's look at today. If I get a quick breakfast, will you get Katrina up and dressed for me? Then we can get away."

By noon they were on the promenade at Yalta, admiring the old buildings with their splendid mouldings and baroque doorcases from around 1910, mixed with the raw newer hotels in Soviet-style economy, thousands of minimal bedrooms and inadequate restaurants. A new five-star luxury hotel was under construction. The sea was placid under a clear sky, a sea of ancient history, of myth and hero and imperial adventure, now the swimming pool of the champion workers.

There was paddling and splashing and laughing, then splendid ice creams and casual shopping. Elspeth bought gifts to take back to Geneva – there were Russian dolls in endless displays – and Niki found a bright blanket embroidered with Cossack designs for Katrina. Then lunch and a drive along the coastal road. Ferries and fishing boats, stalls selling roast potatoes, and at one point a large baritone was entertaining a crowd on the promenade. They turned inland and found orchards, a thriving agriculture scene and a quiet corner where they could lie on the grass and let Katrina roll around, exploring a little world, while they – inevitably, it seemed – held hands, then held each other.

Driving back into the town they hardly needed to discuss the night ahead, and found a guest house well behind the promenade hotels where the heavily bearded manager was unconcerned with details of visas. He waved them into a large bedroom with a couch which could be made up into a bed for Katrina, basic washing in a basin stained with rust and overall a faint smell of frying. It was not a glamour scene but suited their mood and their resources. Niki went out to buy some food, coming back with a package of fish and fried potatoes, which made Elspeth feel much at home, with a tin of mashed vegetables advertised as 'Premium Infants' for Katrina.

It all became easy and natural. They had to be quiet as Katrina slept, so lay on the bed talking of their families and their life journeys. Niki learned that Elspeth came from a Yorkshire family, her father a solicitor in the old town of Selby, south of York, her mother active as a volunteer guide in Selby Abbey, two brothers, with uncles and aunts scattered across northern England. She had gone south to Bristol University to do modern languages, found success in the university hockey team, finished with a first class degree and had thought rather vaguely about finding work as an interpreter. She had a year in France perfecting her accent and idiom but then the opportunity at Geneva was suggested by her uncle the Archbishop. This had seemed ideal, an international community, and the family interest in the church, much more to her liking than another possibility with the European Commission in Brussels.

Niki's story was typically Russian, for his family was torn apart by the war. His parents were killed in an air raid and he had been brought up by a farming uncle. In his teens he had been influenced by a remarkable local priest, who gave him private tuition and encouraged him to study the classics of Russian history. This had led to Moscow and the university course in philosophy and literature, with the usual Marxism emphasis, and there he had met Petrovna. But back home in the country the church appealed, he read theology and was admitted to seminary classes. Friends in Moscow introduced him to the glories of the Patriarchate with its old library, and there he found his true milieu, study, worship, discussion, a world of ideas. He wrote a book on the social theory of Nikolai Berdyaev, whom he admired. The book was a success and this led to his ordination as a deacon, available to teach in church seminaries. He married, taught for four years and then Geneva came along.

Leisurely, quietly, they were learning to know each other, and when they were ready for the night they were at ease to cuddle and gently explore, gasps muffled. It happened with growing confidence, with delight and total giving to each other, bodies joined, no disappointment but strength and fulfilment, both having to be quiet even when longing to shake the bed and shout aloud. They slept, woke early, made love, slept again until Katrina started calling, as the sun flooded into the dingy room, which, in memory, became a sultan's palace.

All Niki's caution was overlaid with gratitude for such a time of intimacy. If it was worship of the flesh, then surely it was no heresy. As they drove through the early morning, both knew that this was no one-night stand. "It's difficult to telephone to Geneva and I can't very well do it from the office, so would you write to me and tell me your news and your thoughts?" asked Niki.

"I'll write, dear Niki, you can be sure of that," said Elspeth, nursing Katrina on her lap. "This has been the best weekend of my life and I'm not about to forget it."

"Don't feel that you have to be entirely silent, and if you want to share, speak with Marion Menzies, for she seemed to me such a wise, straightforward person. But I think we both have to be clear that we have not yet made a long-term commitment. I'm not running away. But I don't want to be just on a rebound, escaping from the loneliness. Can you bear with me?"

"Yes, Niki, for as long as you need. But I am not going to lose you, for I love you. Do you think Katrina likes me?"

"It surely looks like that." Some silence, the road surface rough. Then, "I think I will have to work on your name. Elspeth does not fit into Russian at all well. Elspinova? Elsopetra? Nikolas is easy for you. Now I think this is the road to the airport."

"Too soon. I don't want to say goodbye. But I have to get the flight to Moscow and connect with the regular Geneva Swissair."

At the terminal Niki carried Katrina to the departure gate. They kissed discreetly and Elspeth was waved through. No tears but a wondering heart. Then back to work, driving as quickly as possible to his office, to be met by Timoteo Tachek, who said, "The Bishop wants to see you immediately." He went to the residence and climbed up to the office, where the Bishop waved him in. "Come and sit down, Niki. I just want to sort out a little trouble here. The police office called me to ask whether it was a fact that you were hosting a young Englishwoman this weekend. Is that so?"

"Yes, Bishop, she is an old friend I worked with in Geneva."

"That's fine with me, but the police have been told from higher up that this connection is undesirable and that you must go to the police and make a declaration that it is over."

"I'm sorry, Bishop, but I cannot do that. I think I am likely to become engaged to her. But before we think of what this might mean for the future, can you give me some idea how this comes about? I have tried to do the work as well as I can. I have not been active politically – and as far as I know Elspeth has not been in politics."

"That's very hard for me to answer, but I think the problem is with you rather than with her. You see, Niki, the police in Moscow know all about your Geneva life – you told me once that there was an incident there – and that now you are doing a lot of travelling and keep in touch with the Vatican. So my guess is that they regard you as suspicious, too international, too much adrift from the Russian church, and they don't like it. They regard the church as the private chaplain of the rulers of the state, as it has been in times past. They don't want the church to be the international player; that is for the Kremlin. So they want to curtail you, perhaps to confine you, and to stop this personal association with an English woman could be one way to do that. I may be wrong, but that's my reading of the situation."

"Thanks, Bishop, that makes the position much clearer for me. You think we must take this seriously?

"Yes. I can't see any other reason why they should pick on Archdeacon Nikolas."

"Then it really means that I cannot do this work here properly any longer, and that shocks me. Nor could I do it from Moscow, for to be secretary to the Reconciliation Council really does need freedom to travel. Do you feel it might be good to phone Archbishop Stanislav in Kiev who is my chairman and ask him if he has someone who could take over my work. It is the work that I want to protect – our only chance of crossing the bridge."

"Yes, let's do it straight away."

That conversation, in very guarded tones, produced a positive suggestion. The Archbishop had a couple of capable people who could do at least some of work, though he did not want to lose Niki.

"But now, should I go to the police? What could I say?"

"I wonder if you could say that you have no permanent connection with this Englishwoman and that you are resigning your post here and returning to the Moscow Patriarchate. Would that not be an honest statement? I would come with you and assure them of our good intentions. There's no benefit in making this a case of fighting for our honour."

It was a sensible tactic, for the Bishop was immensely popular in the city as a man with a generous heart who could be trusted to help people in all sorts of desperate need. He gave no ground, did not flatter the police inspector but encouraged Niki to make his statement quite briefly. It was all over in half an hour. There was no arrest warrant. It was as though the Party was just reminding the church who was boss.

A week of intensive packing followed. The office files all had to be carefully boxed and sent off to Kiev, and then the rooms cleaned and handed back to the diocese. Timoteo Tachek was released with a month's pay and no regrets, for it seemed most likely that he had been in touch with the police and had shared details of Niki's work diary with them. No accusation was made but no love was lost.

A message came from Archbishop Stanislav asking Niki if he would remain as a corresponding member of the Council, "for we value greatly your clarity of mind, your intimate knowledge of the process and your emphasis on the main issues." This delighted him; it seemed to authenticate his work. Packing up the home was not complex as he had not accumulated much domestic clutter; one box was devoted to Katrina's needs, one for linen, towels and blankets, and one for the kitchen. Then one for books and pictures and they were done. Clothes would go in suitcases to be carried. The Bishop arranged a cheerful lunch party, with Mrs Rubetz providing a dozen platters of cold meat, tarts and salads, clergy from the cathedral invited and the Bishop's gardener and driver happily engaged near the table.

As the train would be a long trip for Katrina, a flight was booked and so, within so few days, Niki found himself back in the Moscow Patriarchate where a small apartment was prepared and relations with the staff renewed. Patriarch Minchov received him with a welcome which was entirely proper but not cordial, for he was well aware that Niki was in a vulnerable position, providing the authorities with a cause for inspecting church affairs too closely.

"I think that a quiet period of teaching in the seminary would be a good plan for you. It would settle your mind. It would use your talents. You would not need to travel. So please go and consult the Director on the courses."

***

The Secretary of State in the Vatican, Cardinal Jose Sabatini, was making his regular report to Pope Gregory.

"I have some concern, Father, for the work of our brother Cardinal Terracini with the Reconciliation Council. It is indeed a good work, for we all are praying for this great reconciliation with the Orthodox, but it may go too far and too fast. I have heard that the Council is about to discuss the acceptance of married priests as part of the mutual recognition of ministries. Now that is just too much; we cannot go down that road. The rule of celibacy is part of the very fabric of the Church, so I am suggesting to you, Holy Father, that you put the brakes on this adventure."

"I am well aware of the agenda being discussed. I don't see how this question can be avoided, for it was one the causes of division long ago. Whether there can be any progress, any form of conciliation, we shall have to wait and see. But I am not ruling it out. Why would we be afraid of such a discussion? It is not a topic which is based on a word of Christ but on the development of our practice over the centuries, so why be fearful? I do not suppose a revolution is just around the corner, but maybe a suggested way forward."

"Yes, but suggestions become proposals and then there is much publicity and we are pushed onto the defensive."

"But why, my friend, do you think that a married priest is such an impossible channel of grace? Is there not apostolic sanction? And do not the priests of the Orthodox exercise genuine spiritual ministries? Of course it is not our tradition, but I cannot see that is a disobedience to the Gospel."

"Yes, we will wait and see, but I have to say that any radical movement will meet a wave of obstruction and resistance."

"We will face that if it comes. Let us be hopeful that the members of this critical Reconciliation Council can do some good work which we can consider from all points of view. I sometimes wonder if those of us who have worked here in Rome for many years are not isolated from the reality of life for most believers."

"You mean me?"

"I was speaking generally, "said the Pope, smiling. "and I ought to tell you that next month I am going to Turin and then up into the hills to meet a congregation of the Waldensians and I will share in their Sunday worship."

"But they're long ago declared heretical."

"Yes, I know the history. You see, my brother, that I seek to be the one who reaches out beyond the history. Perhaps, if God gives me time, I can enable other parts of the family of Christ to regard the Pope as their bishop or their pastor. That would be a great healing."

"Father, I am not sure that I can serve you in this adventure. I believe that we are called to preserve the holy tradition of the Church, to defend it in difficult times and pass it on in all its glory to another generation. If I am in your way, then I will resign."

"In all its glory? Yes, we both know our church history and we are thankful for all the saints and all the loving service. But we also know the other side, the dark side. Remember the blatant corruptions, the anger, the avarice, the cruelty that was once here, in this place, in your office and mine." He got up and walked about the room, his voice rising. "That's the history that made the Hussites and the Waldenses and the Lollards. It was about this sacred office turned into a political shambles. Those reformers were not fighting against the adoration of

God and obedience to the Christ, but against the moral blindness of those sad years. So we have had to change. I hope we have changed. I intend to show them that this is so. I would hope you can assist me. Please don't rush to conclusions. You will know, as the days go by, whether my intentions are obedient to the Spirit. Now, tell me how you evaluate our South African visit."

***

After six months teaching in the seminary in Moscow, Niki knew that he had to face some hard decisions. Katrina was growing fast and he was unable to give her all the time she needed. The Patriarchate had a supervised play group, but it was not open at weekends or evenings. All the pressures of being a single parent made Niki feel guilty. There was a growing pile of letters from Elspeth, telling him of life in Geneva and her love for him, not wavering for a day. She was so sure of her own mind and heart that she had told her family everything. There was not going to be an easy way out of the walled compound, for Niki realised that once he managed to travel to Geneva he might never be allowed back to the Soviet Union, cut off from his spiritual home. The sickle could slash and the hammer could pulverise without mercy.

There was another element which he pondered. As he had been teaching the history and the theology of the Russian Church since its early days, he realised in a fresh way how subservient it had been to the state. It had been first and foremost the Church of the Czars and only then the Church of the people. The Czars had been close to divinity and the Church had buttressed their self-image. So, in the communist period, there was little other attitude among the senior clergy but to minister faithfully and acceptably to those in power. The regime might be sending millions to the Gulag but the Church was not a protest movement. Render to Caesar.... to Czar or to Commissar.

Niki could not help contrasting this with the attitudes he had found in Geneva, where there was freedom to take up the cause of oppressed people, to publicise political barbarism and to claim that the Gospel of liberation was for all. Of course, that was very risky. Enthusiasm could take the place of understanding. But still it seemed a better witness to the prophetic, radical Christ than the alliance with power. This was not something he could discuss with his elders in Moscow without seeming to criticise their ingrained habit of mind, but he poured it out in letters to Elspeth, who could understand every nuance.

So thoughts of escape occupied his night hours. What might be possible? Train to Minsk and across Poland? Too many borders, too many custom inspections. Fly to Geneva? But they would probably stop him at the airport. Ship across the Baltic? He did not fancy his chances as a stowaway. The best chance of all, it seemed to him, was to arrange a business trip to Kiev at the request of the Archbishop and then to travel with him to the next meeting of the Reconciliation Council in Athens. If the Archbishop would take him as his companion and aide then the police would find it hard to detain him. But what of Katrina? He would not be taking her to a high-level business gathering. Might it be possible for Petrovna's mother to relax from her chilly persona and take the child into her apartment for a while and perhaps find a new warmth in her home? Or would the nuns be better and safer?

With all this churning around in his mind, he made an appointment to see Patriarch Minchov to share his dilemma. "Father, I am torn. I am doing a teaching job here which is going well, but I long to have a family so that my daughter can be properly cared for, and I confess that I long for the freedom of thought that I found in Geneva. There is something energising there, some breeze of the Spirit. We seem to have been built into an unmoveable framework. That is my upbringing and I will never despise it, but somehow I cannot sit easily with it any more."

"That's not hard for me to understand, Nikolas. There is always a tension between new and old, tradition and exploration, the eternal word and the new interpretation. Your work in the last years has led you to move to the more reforming sense of our obedience. But are you sure that a woman is not at the bottom of all this?"

"I have to admit that my English friend Elspeth Beach has something to do with it. I am not yet committed but my heart says that she will be my wife."

"Well, there is nothing that I can say against that, for logic can't win against the passions of the heart. But does this mean that you are looking towards a life in the west?"

"Yes, Father. It is this combination of longing to have a family life and the desire to be of real use in the development of Christian unity. I have a thought about the way I might take and which would need your help, for I know the police would like to trip me up and destroy my future. If you could contact Archbishop Stanislav in Kiev, asking him to send a formal request for me to go there as his personal aide at the next meeting of the Reconciliation Council. That meeting will be in Athens. If I could travel that far in his party, then I think I would be safe to fly on to the west, perhaps with Cardinal Terracini to Rome and then to Geneva. It's a long way round, but seems to me the safest. What do you think?"

"That's rather complex. It might be overkill. For I doubt that you are targeted as such an important individual to be given so much attention. But who can tell with our internal security system. Yes, I'll help you that far. But what about your daughter?"

"I am wondering if the nuns might care for her while I look for a settled job and a home, and then I can send for her."

Practical planning was not difficult; the pieces fell into place. The mental struggle was far more complex. Leaving his homeland under some suspicion, he was not likely to get back again until there should be change in the regime, and that made the journey look like an exile. Could he give up all connection with the work he had been doing with such acceptance, such a sense of fulfilment? He had found Elspeth desirable, exciting company, eager to be at one with him in every part of life, but there was a twelve year gap in their ages and a much wider gap in background. Could that be overcome with love? So he wondered in the night if he was ready for such an adventure when he could keep teaching in the seminary, a rising academic, safe and diligent, for many years. There was confusion between his calling to serve the Christian cause and the basic needs of a human being; could they be bound up together?

The adventure, and the lover, won. Minchov provided the air ticket to Kiev and advised Niki to take a large suitcase. There was no formal farewell, it was to be just a regular business trip. Welcomed by Stanislav in the splendid city mansion, they worked on the agenda for the meeting in Athens a week ahead. Then the Archbishop arranged his party, his chaplain, his personal aide (who was to take over the role that Niki had played for the Council) his secretary – Niki – and his 80 year old mother who had a lifelong desire to see the Parthenon. He warned Aeroflot that they would need a little assistance at the airport. So there was some fussing with a wheelchair, a quick passage to the departure lounge, then the Archbishop asked one of the airport security men to push the wheelchair up the ramp to the plane, where he was graciously thanked and blessed. As the plane took off, the Archbishop was silent, eyes closed, smiling. Niki was elated.

In Athens the Council was busy with its annual report, which had to become a public document, so was examined with great care. Niki had a seat in the background but read all the documents. In a last effort to help things move, he had prepared a piece on the meaning of the papacy in the new relationship and he gave this to Archbishop Stanislav. It may have been dreamland. He had always tried to be a step or two ahead of the discussion.

"THE BISHOP OF ROME, representing the unity of the universal church and respecting the diversity of its local vocation,

Presides at the most senior councils of the international church,

Honours the traditions of devotion and discipleship among Catholics and Orthodox,

Retains authority for the priesthood and for pastoral discipline within the Catholic communion,

Listens to the Word of God in Scripture and to the people of God as they live their faith,

Expresses the challenge of the Gospel to the powers of injustice, greed and death,

Helps the Church to reveal the love of Christ for the poor, sick and abused,

Proclaims the reality of God in the worship of the church, the glory of the natural world and the lives of faithful people,

And welcomes all who love Christ and seek to walk humbly with God."

I wonder, thought Niki, whether that is just for the waste paper basket. I'm sure it is rather too radical for the conservatives and too simple for the theologians, but it is a little hint of what might be born if the Council has enough courage.

9

It was Elspeth who introduced Niki to the mnemonic SUNWAD, part of his introduction to Yorkshire. It stood for the streams which flowed down from the Dales and found their exit in the wide Humber, the Swale, Ure, Nidd, Wharfe, Aire and Don, and it was part of what she remembered from the geography class at school. They had come to Selby, where the Wharfe wriggles its way through the town, so that her parents could meet Niki and see what might become the setting for life together. They came from Geneva with the blessing of Marion Menzies and Walter Schwartz. It was, as ever in these circumstances, a nervous encounter. "A Russian deacon, twelve years older?" worried her mother. "Orthodox clergy of any name, how restrictive," her father was baffled. And in Niki's mind it was the crossing of a long bridge into a foreign culture.

Francis Beach had his office right in the centre of the town, near the abbey, in a handsome late-Georgian building, with the shining brass plate announcing "Beach and Cooper, Solicitors". It was a name unchanged for over thirty years, so had gathered a long list of clients, many family secrets, and a respected place in civic life. Francis was now 58, tall and thin, with swept-back greying hair and light blue eyes behind rimless glasses. Elizabeth was four years younger, comfortably built, still with a country-woman's complexion; she was skilled at the arts of housekeeping, and enjoyed her days on duty as a guide in the abbey. She liked to Sell Selby, as the slogan went.

Both were aware of the English reputation for snobbery and were determined to shine as welcoming parents, even if puzzled by their daughter's love for this Russian, for they knew in their hearts that language and nationality had little to do with the affairs of love. A bit stiff at first – How was the journey? Sorry it's not a sunny day. Let's put the luggage in the garage. Lunch coming up in half an hour. Relax with a sherry. Then four seats at the table and a steaming shepherd's pie put them more at ease.

"We have heard a lot about you from Elspeth," Francis said, "and of course it is all good news, but I wonder what you have in mind to do now – stay in England or work in Europe?"

"First I need to seek your blessing to become engaged to Elspeth so that we may explore the future together. Then I intend to go to the university, which Elspeth tells me is rapidly expanding, to see if there may be a post there for me to teach Russian language and literature. I'm ready to try. You see, I'm a deacon, not a priest, and my work was largely teaching in Moscow."

"What do you think, dear?" Elizabeth wanted to hear it from her daughter.

"Mum, I just want to support Niki and be with him. So I could look at the Modern Languages faculty to see if they want anyone with my qualifications. Or I could take on some translation work for the university press."

"That sounds sensible. We won't stand in your way but give you our blessing. But I do think it's right," Francis sounded professional, "for you to get the employment matter set pretty firmly before you plan a wedding. We will have to think about a work permit; the university could help with that. And now let's have a glass of wine and drink to your engagement."

"And tomorrow, Mum, will you be free to show Niki around the Abbey?"

"Of course, I will make sure of that. I don't want to embarrass you, but what about your sleeping arrangements? Would you like to be back in your old room, dear?"

"No, thank you, Mum. We would like to be together. We phoned through for a room at the Old White Rose in town. I hope you don't mind."

Mum probably did mind, but she hid it well – These young people just have to go their own way.

"Thank you both for your welcome. I know that I'm a rather unusual sort of suitor – you might think I'm a character out of Chekhov – but I'm a widower and a father, so I have to think sensibly about the future, and I'm quite sure in my mind that if Elspeth will have me then I am confident we can make a good future together."

"If we know our own daughter," Dad accepted fate, "she will have said Yes before you have asked the question."

Over the next weeks Niki had an intensive course in English weather, Yorkshire dales, British bureaucracy, Abbey and Minster, Viking relics, Castle Howard and local accents. With Elizabeth as guide he admired the grand nave at Selby and with Elspeth he was astonished at the soaring columns and spaciousness of York Minster, so different from the gilded shrines of Moscow, but holding a peace and blessing of their own. They had tea with her uncle, the Archbishop, Eric Stevenson at Bishopthorpe. Niki produced a letter of introduction from the Patriarch, recommending him for any help he might be able to give to the Church of England in relating to the Orthodox. This was much to the Archbishop's agenda; he could see that York might be able to welcome all Orthodox in the area to the Minster as their spiritual focus. They already had a monthly service for Lutherans. He would talk with the Dean.

The university was a modern complex, with much exposed concrete, but some good design which dispelled the crudity of the surfaces. There was space, with lawns and ponds, much frequented by large family gatherings of ducks, leaving smelly traces on the walkways. The senior staff of the Arts Faculty were interested in the possibility of starting a course in Russian Language and Literature, for there was a push to improve British understanding of such a potential market for British goods, and such a major exporter of oil and gas. More people were needed who could negotiate with Russian firms. And the works of the great Russian writers were treated as essential classics for all students of the nineteenth century literature. But there would be a lot of paperwork to be faced before this possibility could become an engagement. The Home Office would deal with visa and work permit, and the stories of delay were disheartening. The University had its own processes, would need references and details of academic record, so any new course and a new lecturer would be a term away. "But," they said, "there is nothing to stop us inviting you to be a visiting lecturer as a temporary measure as you find your feet." When they found that Niki's book on Berdyaev, translated into English, was in the Faculty library, the pathway seemed assured.

"Are you sure, Niki," asked Elspeth that night, "that you will be content with this little patch of England? You have been such a traveller."

"I can't see very far ahead. But this seems right to me now. I have to find a home for Katrina and a job that I can do. I'm sure, every day, that we should be married. We are so well teamed together. I enjoy you more and more and love to have you close."

"You know my mind and heart. Not one doubt."

"Perhaps travel might come a bit later. We both feel at home in Geneva. But that is very expensive and we'd better be very careful for a while."

So the machines of bureaucracy copied papers and civil servants initialled them, in interviews Niki produced references with impressive commendations from a Patriarch and a Cardinal, the Home Office department in Luna House in Croydon, a sterile and exhausting environment, became familiar, and the Accommodation Office of the University produced a list of possible apartments for their inspection. It was slow work but the signs were that by October they could be settled. Then an invitation arrived from the Dean and Chapter of York Minister for Niki to become an Honorary Canon, with care for Orthodox people and worship. This marked acceptance in a remarkable way and gave the couple confidence that they had made a good choice.

***

Darker shades clouded the Vatican. Pope Gregory was pleased with the response he received when he visited other communions. He knew that the Reconciliation Council was doing sound work, but slowly, how slowly. The Secretary of State seemed to have formed an opposition alliance, with the Spanish and Italian Cardinals and with some of the more conservative Asians and Africans, determined to block the Pope's enterprise. They wanted the pure tradition, unallied and unalloyed. It came to a head when the Pope announced that he would, in six months' time, do a visit to Scandinavia, including time with the Lutheran church leaders there.

Cardinal Jose Sabatini was skilled at manipulating the Vatican diplomatic corps. He sent messages to the papal nuncios in the four Scandinavian countries, suggesting that they advise the Pope to cancel, or at least delay, his visit. "I think you are aware of plans for a major foreign leader to visit Scandinavia at about that time, and so the security services would not be able to deal properly with a Papal visit. Also we have strong reasons for ensuring that the Holy Father be in the Philippines at that time. It would be helpful if you could communicate with the Pope's secretary in such terms."

In his regular meeting with the Secretary of State, Gregory needed information. "I have word advising me to cancel my visit to the Scandinavian church and this is the first time that a proposed visit has not been warmly welcomed. Do you know anything about this?"

"Holy Father," replied the Secretary of State, "I know our people there and they are very sound, experienced men, so I am sure that their advice is wise. I suggest you put that visit into the Pending list."

"But that does not quite answer my question. Are you against the visit?"

"Yes, Holy Father. It is my conviction that it would right for the life of the Church that you should concentrate on visits to our own community. It is not our business to spend precious time and energy and publicity on lunching with Lutherans. They have their own leadership. We have to tend the flock that God has given to us. That's a big enough task to absorb your ministry."

"I have a different sense of my office, that it is to become a focus of unity for the wider Christian community in the world, and that this is what we have to seek in the few years that I have in this life to affect the course of events. If you seriously want to challenge this, then I do not think we can work together."

"I will take 24 hours to think about it. I will tell you tomorrow how best I can respond."

Both men were disturbed, both conscientious, both toughened through many years of church politics and now seriously divided. One was staunchly traditional, operating in time honoured fashion to preserve the familiar structures and doctrines. This was not an evil intent, but blinkered by that defensiveness which pervades all ancient institutions. The other realised that the influence of his position could be channelled into reform; that meant some risk, some uncertainty but also some new life. As Secretary of State, Sabatini was able to sound out most of the senior colleagues and found that there was widespread impatience with the Pope's agenda, when there were so many urgent issues to be dealt with about the priesthood, the religious communities, the rising power of Islam, the mixture of faith and superstition in Africa and the breakdown of marriage in the west. So he quickly came to the conclusion that it was not for him to retire, but for the Pope to change his priorities.

In his lonely apartments, Pope Gregory had few confidants, but many officials. They groomed him, fed him, presented the daily stack of papers, detailed his diary, suggested his sermons, guarded his privacy and organised his finances. Like royalty he was privileged but constrained. Terracini from Milan and a few others from North America and Western Europe were supporting his efforts, but with carefully restrained publicity, for they too had pressure from conservatives for whom ecumenism was a distraction, a minor hobby.

The stand-off between them continued for some months, neither willing to give ground. There was some bitter gossip around the Vatican as many of the staff became aware of it; "not the good feeling we used to know." Gregory rejected any thought of resignation; his vocation, he was sure, had to be followed, whatever the opposition.

He was walking in the well-tended private garden, the camellias just coming into flower, the late afternoon sun bringing out the sparkle on the dome of St Peter's, his secretary at a distance, not interrupting his meditation. A figure in dark clothes slipped round the bushes, fired a shot, darted back into the shadow, climbed an aluminium ladder to the top of the wall, left the ladder in place and dropped down among the slender trees. He walked away, soon becoming part of the streetscape in the dusk.

The Pope's secretary heard the shot, did not know what it was, but saw the white figure flat on the ground. He rushed to the Pope's side. There was a growing, glaring scarlet stain, a shocking contrast, on the pure white fabric. Unsure what to do, he ran to the nearest guard-post shouting for help. In a minute the Swiss guard and the domestic staff were on the scene, anxiously trying to assess how serious was the wound. He was breathing, but very weakly and his colour looked deathly. Within five minutes the medics were there with a stretcher and an ambulance was at the gate, and a dash, with blaring klaxons, to the hospital. From the emergency room the news filtered out, the Pope was severely wounded in the lungs, internal bleeding severe, his breathing feeble and erratic, his condition critical.

While the press gathered at the hospital, the police were calling up their full strength to watch the railway station, the airport, the major roads out of town – but looking for what? They had no description. As always the police looked impressive; Italian style mattered. The state security bureau was called on by the Prime Minister to examine all known threats to His Holiness. The Vatican, and the Vatican watchers, hovered in disbelief.

The Swiss guard soon picked up the ladder, handled it with gloves, and identified it as belonging to the maintenance department. One of their three ladders was missing from its place in the storeroom. Was any member of staff missing? There were urgent calls to those off duty, but no absentees. All were to be grilled the next day. The police took the ladder for intensive fingerprinting. They found many prints and a lot of smudging, but all appeared to be matched to members of the maintenance staff. There was a quick round up of the most active terrorist suspects, their alibis probed, but no leads. It looked very much like an inside job.

The Italian press, with its normal ignorant enthusiasm, produced its boldest headlines. POPE CRITICAL POPE STABLE PRAY FOR POPE POLICE HAVE SUSPECT NO LEADS YET THE WORLD WATCHES. The terrorist probably came from Libya. Authorities believe the attack was planned in Chechnya. Mafia likely to be involved.

Ilya Venich made his way on his efficient little motor scooter to the railway station at Cisterna, south of Rome on the Naples line. He left the machine in a side street. He bought a ticket to Naples; there were no police in sight. He left the slow train at Caserta, bought a ticket to Foggia, and laid up there for a night in a cheap hotel, rising early and catching the first train south to Bari. The port was busy, especially the Molo San Vito, the ferry wharf. Venich wandered around the waterfront, enjoyed some tasty Italian sausage by the Castello and checked the police and customs procedures as the busloads of tourists made their way onto the Dubrovnik ferry.

He was looking for the smaller boat which would sail overnight to the grey, grimy port of Durres in Albania. It did not look difficult. The queue of passengers, laden with bulky cases, bags and parcels of Italian goods, was passed easily through the system. Venich had his Albanian passport and had thrown his revolver out of the train window in the mountains, so had no trouble with the Customs or the Xray. The only item which might have interested the police, had they searched, was a pair of fine cotton gloves, a rather odd embellishment for a rugged, unshaven 25-year-old Albanian.

At Durres he caught the bus to Tirana, and over a few days hitched his way north to Kosovo. There the long, bitter feuding between the people of Albanian origin and the Serbs meant a scene of frequent violence, with the United Nations intervening to keep the peace, with limited success. Venich joined his brother with the Albanian troops.

Both had been inspired – or indoctrinated – by a religious zealot at school, who taught them the history of the Crusades. Never, so they learned, had justice been done to the Popes who had preached and organised war. One day the account must be paid, the lord of the infidels crushed. Ilya let this teaching take control of his life, his ambition, his dreams. So ignorance becomes energy and eight hundred years of history is compressed into monomania and fresh cruelty is born.

It was while he was on the ferry that Pope Gregory had died. Fluttering between life and death, the internal bleeding not controlled, he had been barely conscious for 24 hours, unable to express any last wishes, tended by the best doctors, given the last rites by his personal chaplain. Then the eulogies began. "This most generous and thoughtful of Popes." "The Pope who embraced all Christians." "The Pope who built bridges." Crowds flocked to St Peter's Piazza, many in tears. The full Vatican apparatus turned to funeral preparation, with the Secretary of State in charge of arrangements, appointing himself the principal speaker. Cardinals floated in from all parts of the world and hoteliers were delighted with full occupancy. But the puzzle remained. Was it all an internal affair? Was there a traitor in the ranks? Or was this a Communist plot or a Moslem attack? Or just a crazy loner?

The police, under great pressure from the President of the Republic, the Prime Minister, the press and the radio hosts, concentrated on one of the gardening staff, Jose Marinetti, who had been heard muttering curses on the hierarchy because the church had denied a proper funeral for his son who had committed suicide. Disturbed, he certainly was. But there was not one piece of evidence that could be held against him. Interpol issued a general but vague plea for watchfulness at all the exit borders from Italy, and reviewed its own listing of highly motivated activists.

It took only two days for the left-wing press to start a conspiracy theory. "Who inside the Vatican wanted the Pope to go? Who resisted his reform agenda? Who had easy access to the garden?" So rumours floated around a hundred coffee tables and a thousand bars. Could it all have been a plan of the conservatives? The failure of the police to produce a suspect gave the rumours added impetus.

News of the killing had powerful effects. Cardinal Terracini in Milan was angry and disappointed, his leader, colleague and inspirer swept away, his commission inevitably weakened. President Rubetsky in the Kremlin, accustomed to the removal of leaders, was not greatly surprised or troubled, but sent condolences. Patriarch Minchov was secretly relieved that he would not have to carry forward reforms that could be too upsetting for the faithful. The World Council of Churches office in Geneva was in genuine mourning, for the staff knew that they had lost the man who really could have shifted the ecumenical movement into a higher gear. And for Niki and Elspeth it was devastating; they realised at once that it would be most unlikely that the next pope would share Gregory's priorities. Their work over the last few years could well be shelved or wiped off the map.

Yet they could not remain depressed, they were too young, too well settled into a new life together and too excited by the expected arrival of two nuns with Katrina, carried with care on a flight from Moscow. The nuns were to do study in the Old Testament and Hebrew language at Oxford. Katrina was to be cuddled and bathed and enjoyed in the apartment which the university had suggested, within walking distance of the campus, where Elspeth was busy with a French-to-English translation of a book on the Fin-de-Siecle writers in Paris and London.

A few days later Niki was philosophical about the Pope. "You see, darling, I think I have been rather naïve. I was flattered to be with those splendid church leaders. I was thrilled to be at Sancta Sophia for that great day. I felt that I was contributing to a seriously big work of the Spirit. But perhaps it was fated from the start. Would Gregory ever have been able to carry the Cardinals with him? Maybe I was deluding myself."

"You need not think that. It was a good work and you did very well at it. To have shared in it is a plus and not a minus. We have to wait to see what happens next. There may be good news to come."

"Yes, of course that's right. But I have been thinking about the whole approach. We concentrated on the senior people in the churches, on the basis that they could move things along, they had the power. But perhaps we should be starting at the other end, with the faithful people in all the congregations. Could there be a movement from the ground up?"

"I don't know; it would need a lot of education and organising. Let's just think about it for a bit and see if we get any bright ideas.

But, Niki, in the meantime, we have a wedding to organise. That's my priority. Mother is sure it must be in Selby Abbey and I go along with that. I'd like Uncle Eric to lead the service, so it means finding a date in his calendar. Will you ring his secretary or should I do it?"

"That must be for you – a clear family duty. As soon as you can get a date – the earlier the better – I will call Selby and ask them to start the local preparations. Or you could go down by bus and have a day with your mother."

***

In Moscow the President was evaluating his assured supporters. He could count on the army. As an old army man he knew the generals, their indiscretions, tactical errors and indifference to the wretched conditions of recruits. So he had levers there. With the party hierarchy he was not so sure. Perhaps half of the Politbureau wanted stability more than change, and he could offer that, but among the others some radical ideas were being floated, suggestions that the party was too tired, too inflexible ever to take advantage of new technology and a liberated economy, and so to offer any real competition to the United States. And as for the Church, that was an empire within the empire, its business still wrapped in mystery and its influence beyond the reach of the KGB. His relations with Minchov, the Patriarch had not improved, for there was no trust between them and gradually the President knew himself to be devalued, perhaps despised, by the bearded cleric.

On the platform overlooking Red Square at the great army parades, Rubetsky looked the part in his military uniform, a craggy face beneath the flat cap, but in private he was uncertain, erratic in policy and risky in friendship. When Minchov asked for a private meeting he delayed it for a month and then received him very formally, not like the confidential priest of tradition. The Patriarch was objecting to a variety of insults which he said had upset the Church. The party had punished the priest in one area by imposing a heavy tax on all the church land, and all the priest had done was to preach that Marx and the party doctrine were not the answer to our deepest fears. In another place the city authorities had refused to help the Church with scaffolding to repair the dome, which had been accepted practice for generations. In Moscow itself a congregation had been cleared out of the building during the sacred Eucharist on the charge that fire regulations were not approved. It was plain that the tolerance of the State for the Church was descending into active opposition. "Is that your policy, Mr President?"

"My responsibility is to guard the strength of the nation. Everything else is secondary. If I see the Church as an irritating rash on the skin or as an infestation of the gut, then I will act appropriately. If the Church stays in its place and attends only to its own business, then it will survive."

"We are approaching the anniversary of the end of the Great Patriotic War, Mr President, when we shall remember the heavy losses, the mourning and the bravery. We were both young at the time. I think you were in the army, serving with the advanced infantry as a stores officer. I wonder if you have seen this old photo of the soldiers with no proper boots, but with strips of blanket tied round their feet."

"I am aware of the privations of that time."

"And I am aware of the army trucks that came to our village and unloaded crates of army supplies."

"What are you suggesting?"

"Only that we might be more understanding of each other. It is not for me to act as a judge."

"Then don't threaten me. I'll have you squashed like a beetle if you do."

"No threats, Mr President. But just a reminder that we are all imperfect people. We all need forgiveness. I speak as a priest. So I ask you to allow the Church to fulfil its calling with freedom."

"Yes, but freedom only within the limits of security for the State. I decide those limits. That is what you would call my vocation."

A buzzer was pressed, aides entered, the Patriarch was ushered out of the presence.

It was that afternoon that President Rubetsky made the most foolish decision of his life. He realised that he had two options. He could go to the Patriarch, make a full confession of his time as a Stores

Officer in the war, seek absolution and become a child of the church, under the thumb of the clergy. Or he could show who was boss. He unthinkingly chose the latter. He ordered the General of the Moscow District Command to put a light tank and a platoon of guards at the splendid gatehouse of the Patriarchate, with instructions to examine the credentials of all visitors, detaining any who were known to the police as dissidents.

Word quickly spread. People stopped on the street and stared, photos were secretly taken, reports were whispered in the efficient way of the underground. But what was it all about? All that could be guessed was that some dissident was seeking asylum in the compound or some terrorist threat against the Church had been uncovered. No-one, other than Minchov, knew that this was the President's response to his interview, revealing the President's desperate need to control events and prevent a leak of his past history to the foreign media. Through the Church network, Minchov was able to inform all the bishops that the army was harassing the sacred precincts. It took a couple of weeks to gather the faithful into an effective opposition, but then they poured into the Moscow streets, many thousands, blocking roads, coming in from all sectors, stopping traffic, raising the cross, chanting the old psalms. They stood, they sang, they sat on the roads, they filled Red Square. Although the older religious people formed the nucleus of the crowd, they were joined by thousands of students who were frustrated by the party orthodoxy of the teaching in all the universities, by smallholders unable to sell their produce at any profit, by the artistic community longing for some scope for adventure, and by crowds of others who were ground down by the gross inefficiency of the regime. "Must be a hundred thousand," muttered the city mayor. "More like half a million," said the General.

"Clear the streets. Do it now." The President's order was unambiguous.

But as the army units met the crowds, they could not drive tanks through the mass of people sitting on the road. The soldiers saw the Orthodox cross held high by a robed priest and refused to shoot. It was passive mutiny. The Central Committee of the Party gathered as best they could and argued through the night. They heard that at two places the soldiers had joined the crowd and let the students clamber over the tanks. Rubetsky pleaded for steady military control – "They will fade away when they get hungry." The majority of the members saw him as the sacrificial lamb. Throw him to the mob. "He's had his time; let him go."

Next morning the broadcast news bulletin announced that the President had resigned. He was to be succeeded by Ivan Markovic, a civilian, a doctor of anthropology, a progressive, a well-known writer on the history of the land, who was known to be on the fringe of the Party and a regular church attender. He had been dragged from his bed during the night and called to do his duty. With great reluctance he went out to the viewing platform on the Kremlin wall and spoke to the crowd.

"I salute you, the people of Moscow. You have shown courage. I salute you, the army. You have shown mercy. I salute you, the clergy. You have shown faith. I am here not because I want to be and not because I have any ambitions to hold power, but because I have been called to serve you, and to serve our great nation.

I am committed to ensure that the nation is governed by law and not by the army or the personal whim of any politician. We will respect the Church, for we are all God's children. We will all speak freely our ideas and plans and hopes. Nobody should be punished for speaking or publishing an honest opinion. We will have a general election as soon as possible to elect a new National Assembly. We must give everyone the chance to earn a decent living.

This is the direction I will take. You must judge whether we travel well. Now let the army return to barracks. And you all can go home and tell your children that today you have made history."

There was cheering like waves of noise around the square, much waving of flags and a drift to the Metro stations. The crisis was over. But that was simply to announce that new struggles would begin.

***

In Rome the ceremonies and the enquiries occupied the public conversation. Nobody could do a state funeral as well as the Vatican. There was genuine grief, but this was overlaid with a flamboyant carpet of scarlet robes, of incense, chanting and processions, all done with slow, precise steps so that formality triumphed over emotion. It was not hypocrisy but habit. It was about as far from the disciples at the Tomb in the Garden as it is possible to be. And when the Cardinals assembled three days later in the Sistine Chapel for the vital conclave, the observer would have seen prayerful men at prayer, seeking the leading of the Holy Spirit, as though no political thought had occurred to them when considering the choice to be made.

In the eulogy at the funeral the Secretary of State had stressed the courage of Gregory. "We saw a leader of the people of God, one who stood in the tradition of the apostles, utterly faithful to his Lord. He knew his calling and, despite disappointment, held to it with ability and grace. He went ahead of us. He broadened our horizons. He was truly a worldwide Father in God. We, who stood close to him, knew a humble man, never imperious, at work early and late, frugal in his habits. We feared that he, as he moved far beyond the routine of office, might leave us behind, but that was his pattern of leadership and we praise God for it. Now today, we offer his life and his work to our heavenly Father, with thanksgiving and confidence, as this good Gregory leads us, in very truth, far beyond our human horizon."

All agreed that it was a very suitable address, in impeccable Latin. It carried a clear message that another such leader might indeed travel out of sight of the faithful. It contained not one word about the killing or the assassin or judgement.

That investigation was under the command of Commissario Julio, a respected senior officer who had recently solved the murder of a society hostess and so won the approval of the Minister of Police. He ordered another check of all the Vatican employees, their location at the time of the killing marked on a big map of the Vatican, and their alibis noted against each other. He was looking for the weak link which allowed a stranger to be in the private garden. The routine was for the Swiss Guards to check the gardens half an hour before the closing time of the museum, ushering all late visitors to the exit. It was only after that that the Pope had been walking that afternoon. It became clear that workmen and gardeners were often putting their tools away, chatting in groups, changing out of overalls, having a smoke, all in a very casual way, so that during the critical half hour a careful intruder could easily slip into the shadows of the bushes. That, Julio knew, was how it was done, but was no closer to knowing the identity of the gunman.

It was not until two weeks after the murder that Julio read, among the mass of reports telling of suspicious strangers lurking, so it seemed, in every town in Italy, a small note from the sergeant of police at Cisterna. "Reporting that a motor scooter was abandoned, no claimant coming forward, so regarded as lost property; but found just two minutes' walk from the railway station." Julio read it as a useless bit of trivia, but reflected that evening that it could be that a fugitive would not use the city railway stations but find a way to somewhere less guarded, so he phoned Cisterna and asked for the scooter to be carefully handled and covered up until his own men arrived to take possession of it.

They were there next morning. They lifted the scooter into the back of their van, signed a receipt for it, and drove back to headquarters. The call then went out to all dealers and garages, quoting the serial and registration numbers, asking if this machine had been sold, hired or given away recently. A day later there was a response from a small dealer in second-hand machines in the Nomentano district, near the Tiburtina station. He was not sure but the registration number seemed familiar. He was brought in to headquarters. Julio went down to meet him and took him to the underground car park where the scooter was kept for a thorough fingerprinting.

"Yes," said the dealer, a short, untidy figure, "I'm sure this is the one. You see it's had a lot of wear and has not been well looked after. There's rust on the mudguards. The electrics are a bit dodgy. The rear tyre does not look at all safe to me"

"How did the man pay for it?"

"In cash. It really was a cheap machine."

"Describe the man as best you can."

"Slim, dark, a leather jacket and jeans. He did not have much Italian and I asked him where he came from. Turkey, he said. Are you going far, I asked him. No, he said, just around the city. That's all we said. He took the receipt and drove off. That's all I can tell you."

Not much to go on there, thought Julio. Back in his office he phoned the police at Cisterna, asking them to enquire at the station whether there was a record of tickets sold at the critical dates. Yes, he was told, it is done automatically but the records are all wiped at six monthly intervals and the summary only is kept in hard copy. But for south-bound passengers you can be pretty sure that ninety per cent are tickets for Naples; just occasionally a party for the Pompeii stop or for Salerno but nothing further south. The clerk could not remember any individual passengers two weeks earlier. Indeed, when the ticket machine was working properly, he rarely met the passengers at all. It seemed like another dead end.

Across the Adriatic in Kosovo there was continual scrapping, sniping and bombing in a disorganised way that tested and often bewildered the UN peacekeepers who could never forecast where the next incident might happen. The Venich brothers were irregulars, joining in local engagements with daring and accurate fire, but never staying very long with each unit. At one half-destroyed village, Ilya clambered into the shell of a two story building and onto the first floor for a better view, treading carefully on the old timber flooring which looked unstable. The Serbs were only a hundred metres away, across a small stream. Ilya watched for thirty minutes, saw them creeping down to the stream, aimed carefully and shot the leading man, reloaded and shot another. But as he then withdrew the rifle, there was a crack, the floor gave way in a great cloud of dust, he fell to the ground still holding the rifle, which swung out of control above him so that the butt slammed into his head just above the right ear. He was out for the count. His brother came looking for him as the Serbs were advancing, found him unconscious on the floor with blood seeping from the wound on his skull.

Two Albanians staggered into the old house. The three men together lifted Ilya as carefully as they could and carried him back to the orchard on the steep hillside, laid him on the grass and attempted a rough bandage round his head. Suddenly a whole troop of Serbs appeared, effectively surrounding them. They shot their way out as they retreated, causing considerable damage, but could not carry Ilya. All they knew, when they had reached a stone wall that gave some shelter, was the confident shouting of the Serbs and then a single shot. For them all, it was a dead end.

***

The Sistine Chapel, the scene for the papal election, had always been a glory of our humanity in the shadow of our mortality; creation above and judgement below. The assembled cardinals shared in both, for they had to be creative in their thinking about the direction for the next papacy but also aware of the frailty of our lives and our judgement. There were natural groupings. The solid block of Italian cardinals preferred one of their number who knew the working of the Vatican. But they were divided between Sabatini, the Secretary of State and Terracini of Milan. As a result, both names dropped out on the second day of the conclave. The cardinals from Asia and Africa looked for the most likely of the candidates from the poorer countries, agreeing to name Alberto Guterrez of Mexico, a man in his sixties who was known to have befriended people trapped in the drug wars and convicts in the wretched prisons. But they had not calculated on the North Americans for whom Mexicans meant feuding illegals, and who would look to one of their own. Their candidate was Pierre Cadeaux of Quebec, now seventy, known as a strict disciplinarian who was not afraid to dismiss misbehaving priests, but had a popular approach as a communicator, often appearing on television, a conservative in theology but liberal in his thinking about the changes in human society. On the third day of the conclave this was the name that cleared every hurdle and sent the white smoke up the chimney.

The crowds in the piazza cheered, the figure appearing on the balcony declared,"Habemus papam" and then Cadeaux came to the microphone, his first words in French, greetings to you all, pray for me, then in English and finally a Latin benediction.

***

10

It was his first winter in Yorkshire. Conversation often started with people telling Niki how cold it could it could be – The east winds come straight from the Ural mountains, you know – as though a man from Moscow had not experienced a real winter. The wedding in Selby Abbey was on a fine autumn day. Since he had no family to support him, Niki invited colleagues and students to share the day. Elspeth spent the wedding eve with her parents, who ensured that she was splendidly dressed in a white trouser suit with a peacock blue shirt under the white jacket. Niki was in black, forthright, assured. Together they were the photographer's delight. No couple could have given more convinced vows before a smiling archbishop. Work at the university was going well, with a keen group of students who found the Russian language full of challenges and the literature magnificent. They were reading a scene from The Cherry Orchard and writing essays on Dostoyevsky and the Russian spirit. There was talk of a party doing a Baltic cruise next summer. The work came readily to Niki and he had time to join the university Chorale, for he enjoyed singing. He was welcomed by the choir leader who grabbed the chance to tackle some Russian church music quite new to them. He asked Niki to give them an introduction to this style of singing.

"I am not at all an expert," he said to them, "but I can pass on what my first teacher said, for it sticks in my mind. The first thing was about the balance of voices. Think of the sea shore, with the waves breaking. That is the constant background. You hear the pulse of it, it is clear, not muffled, but it doesn't shout at you. Then the solo voice, the lead singer is heard over the waves, rather as a descant voice might be in western tradition. The lead singer is not a soloist, not a performer, but just one member of the choir – there might be several of them chosen from time to time – and we have to keep a balance between the strength of the waves of sound and the clarity of the one voice above them.

The second instruction was that when we learn a new piece, we will take it at a faster pace than on the score. That makes it easier to learn. We will do it repeatedly till we have it in our minds. Then we will take it slower and slower, which is much more difficult for the breathing, until it is the slow marching step right for the liturgy.

Of course you know that Russian church choirs were always men only. More recently there have been some choirs of women and some of mixed voices. So you will have to decide whether traditional pieces will be for the men only or will be re-arranged for the whole choir. I think that this can be done quite readily, but it needs a sensitive arranger to keep the balance of voices.

I think that is all that I can share from my experience. I hope you enjoy it."

They tackled it with enthusiasm and certainly enjoyed it. At the end of term concert they offered a mixed programme with three short Russian pieces. Elspeth came and was delighted to see Niki in a new role among the bass voices, obviously among friends. As the students left for the Christmas break, Niki was reflecting on his ease in settling into the York scene. He had found it a straightforward transition. But then, he had found the same thing at Geneva. He realised that he was an accommodating character, readily feeling at home. It was not that he changed like a chameleon, he was still the same man, careful, steady, concerned with ideas, a trusted companion, with the same charming smile, but never stepping out beyond the polite discourse, not a challenger to upset society. Even when he had been writing radical suggestions in his committee work, he was ready to submit them to superiors, who, he knew, would be unlikely to accept them. Indeed, he realised that these senior clerics would not be changed by any committee report, however brilliant. It would take some personal experience, some confrontation to do that. He knew he would never become a big name. Too intelligent to pretend, Niki was glad to follow his academic life as an honest practitioner who was not like some ambitious colleagues, always pushing their barrow of attention-grabbing opinion on television.

But he knew Elspeth was of a different tribe. She had energy and enthusiasm in plenty. She suggested and planned the steps in Katrina's approach to an infant school. She was an exciting lover, physically alert and generous. Her father was right when he had said that she would answer Yes before she heard the question. She would not remain a sheltered homekeeper in a small apartment for ever, but would launch out is some new direction. One day she declared that she had this in her mind.

"Do you remember saying that perhaps we have to stop relying on the top people to make big change possible and find a way of energising the parish congregations?"

"Yes, I remember. I still think that's the way it will have to go, some groundswell."

"Well, I've been thinking. You know that in all the denominations now the small group is very much the thing. They all have their prayer groups and Bible study groups and discussion groups. This helps people to know each other and share their knowledge and faith and doubt. Well, I think we are the ideal people to prepare a series of little study guides on the varieties of Christian church life. Imagine that for each of the major communions we prepare a series of, say, two to four weekly studies. For each week there might be four pages of text, a page or two of discussion material, a page or two of pictures. Then the group leader could use that, knowing that it was sound, not just promotional material. We might call the project Meet the Family. Do you get the idea?"

"Yes, it sound great. You have big thoughts. But how could we ever get it published and advertised?"

"That is where our work at Geneva might be a blessing. I can see Marion Menzies loving the idea, and if the World Council gave us some backing then it could be advertised world-wide."

"Have you thought of everything, darling? Who is going to do all the writing? Of course I can do the Orthodox, but could either of us do a good piece on Methodists or Baptists or the Church of Scotland, or the Moravians?"

"No, we would have to look for authors. But, you know, clergy are always delighted to be asked to write something, they are all authors in hiding."

"Yes," he laughed, "I think you are right. Let us just keep thinking if it is practical."

Elspeth, who had nearly finished the translation of a dull French book, was well ahead in her thinking. They would do a mock-up with the Orthodox as the subject, just to see what it might look like. They would list the whole spectrum of subjects, from which groups could select those most applicable for their context. And they could suggest names of possible authors. She was already thinking of how they would sell the booklets – surely not from their apartment, that was too small. Some storage would be needed. She phoned her mother. "Mum, do you think there might be any room around the Abbey where we could do some packing and mailing of material? It's about a new scheme we have to publish some booklets on the various churches." She would make enquiries. Where would the printing be done? In Yorkshire or abroad? Hong Kong was cheaper.

So it was not long before there was a business plan and a production plan, all of it rushing Niki along like the busy tug pulling the freighter out of harbour to the uncertain ocean.

"This is your project, dear. I will do all I can but I must put the university work first. You are the manager and the editor. It will look rather good – Editor: Elspeth Demenchov. But before you get too far I think there are some important matters to deal with. Will the World Council back this? Perhaps you will need to fly to Geneva and discuss it. Then you must have proper legal standing, some commercial status, if you are going to sell lots of these sets. Could you ask your Dad about that? You see, dear, we have not got the sort of money to pay for rather complex printing and advertising."

"That's true, Niki. But we will get there, I'm sure of it."

"Here's my first effort to describe the Orthodox. It came out as three parts, the first on how the Orthodox developed in the east and spread in Greece and Russia. The second on what the worship and the regular sacraments of the church are like. And the third on current matters, the diaspora, relations with the state and the tension with modernity – you know, tradition versus socialism. I've added some discussion points. Here's the first one. 'The Orthodox stand up for worship, as respect for the presence of the holy. How do we show such respect and reverence when we meet for worship?'"

"This is going to be great. You are wonderful to go along with my wild ideas."

"I've come to love your ideas. But don't leap too far ahead."

But she leapt, made an appointment in Geneva and flew to see Miriam, taking with her a mock-up of the first issue of Meet the Family. Welcomed in the office with hugs and kisses, she told Miriam her vision and of Niki's thoughts on starting with the grass roots rather than the hierarchs. As she talked, her plans grew larger. "After Meet the Family we could go on to Meet the Relatives, about Christian Science, the Adventists and Mormons and so on, and then to Meet the Neighbours, about the other great faiths." Miriam grasped the educational value of small group work and loved the project. "But," she said, "I doubt if the World Council could take it on, for our publishing department has not been doing very well and recently lost a good deal of money on a history of the ecumenical movement. Also the costs of production here are hitting the roof. So I think we could certainly give you our commendation, and advertise in our magazines, but not take on the business risks. Do you see the point."

"Of course, Miriam. That is what I expected and hoped for. Where do you think it would be best to go for the printing?"

"Well, there's no doubt that India is the cheapest. But the quality is not always guaranteed. I think that Singapore or Hong Kong would probably win on quality and price. Look, I'll note for you the local ecumenical contacts, and when you have some more mock-ups and can judge the quantity of the order, they will be able to quote some prices."

"Miriam, it's so good to talk. You can see exactly what is in my mind. Do you think it might work?"

"Yes, I do. You are right that all the churches are doing a lot of work in small groups, so if you can interest the education people in the church offices, then I think it will work well. Just a minute. The biggest market would be in America. It is several times bigger than Europe for this sort of enterprise. Somehow you ought to be in touch there. Here's my contact in the National Council of Churches, he's in Philadelphia."

Spurred on by this hour with Miriam, Elspeth flew home and at once phoned her father and arranged to see him on a business matter at his office. Again she expounded her plans. "Dad, what we need to know is how we could deal with the business side of this. We don't have money to start it going. What could we do to raise that money? Is it simple to form a company?"

"I think it would be a private company, dear, not one listed on the Stock Exchange, and that would not be difficult. We would need to set it up legally with a business address and a list of those putting up the capital. They would have to know that there was a risk. But I don't think you would need a great deal of money to get going – perhaps 10,000 pounds would see you through the first production and distribution. I'm sure your mother and I would put up half of that if you can find the other half. What do you say to that?"

"You are wonderful, Dad. Thanks for trusting me. Please tell me if I am going too fast – Niki thinks I often run when I ought to walk."

"Well, listen to him. I have come to like him more and more and I'm glad he's part of our family."

Elspeth, still full of ideas, made contact with the Rowntree Educational Trust, an offshoot of the old chocolate firm, whose Quaker origins led to a deep engagement with social welfare. Yes, they were interested. Then she tried the York diocesan office to talk to their business manager, but not much hope there, their budget too tight. Still busy, she thought of the Catholic schools department, and there struck gold. They would be very interested in such a series of booklets which teachers could use throughout their school system. And, yes, they would be ready to share in the initial funding. A month later, Elspeth was able to show her father that she had more than enough for the half share of the capital. She reported her success to Niki.

"You are really a wonder, doing all this so quickly. But I have not been asleep. This afternoon I went to have a chat with the York University Press people. You know, they generally do theses and academic books, but they have recently been branching out into creative writing and some course materials for distance learning. I showed them what we have in mind. I asked if they would be interested in doing the production for us and the answer was very positive. That would mean that we would take to them the raw material and the concept. They would design the product, submit it to us for approval, and then go ahead with whatever print run we order. Look, dear, this is the sort of cost they thought would be likely."

"That's not too bad. And the great advantage would be having it all done so close at hand. We would have a bit more control than going all the way to Hong Kong. You are a wonder, too, Niki. Give me a kiss."

***

In the Vatican Pierre Cadeaux, who had kept his own name Peter for his papal title, invited Commissario Julio to give him a briefing on the murder investigation, with the new Secretary of State and his personal secretary taking notes.

"I am not used to such an audience, Your Holiness, so please forgive me if I use the wrong language. But we have been busy, the case is still open and we do not yet have a suspect in custody. We have tracked the murderer. So I can say that it looks like a single, deluded individual and not an organised group killing. The man, we can call him Mr X, learned the routine of the gardens and museums at closing time. He saw that the easiest way to escape the guards was to wait for that half hour before the closing when the guards were clearing the visitors from the grounds and then to slip in by the workmen's gate as the men were packing up, with no thought but getting home to a good evening meal. He had bought a cheap scooter and parked that ready for his getaway outside the wall not far from the old railway station. Dressed like one of the workmen he took a ladder from the store to that spot on the wall and hid in the thick shrubs there. After the deed he climbed over the wall, walked to the road where the scooter was and drove quietly south out of the city before our police could close the roads.

He reached Cisterna. Parked the scooter in a side street and caught the train going south. I am pretty sure that he bought a ticket to Naples but got off the train at Caserta and switched to the line going to Foggia, where we now know he spent the night. He left next morning. I have no proof but I have a strong conviction that he went south to Bari for a ferry connection. We have not been able to track him with any confidence there. But all the signs are that he was a person from either the Balkans or the Middle East and saw stowing-away on a ferry as the best way out of Italy. From the descriptions of his appearance and accent I would say that he probably came from Turkey or Albania. I see him as a deluded, perhaps mentally-disturbed man with a conviction that he had to do this deed for his faith or as some kind of revenge for some ancient wrong. There is a red alert issued by Interpol. But with the present disturbances in the countries across the Adriatic, you will understand that to locate a single man is very difficult, as the police there have major problems to deal with. Sir, that is as far as we have got to date."

"You have done very well, Commissario. Thank you for your persistence. I am sure you will have indicated to the Swiss Guard where the gap was in their security, so that can be dealt with. And it is something of a relief to know that the murder was not a conspiracy, with all this Mafia rumour flying around in the press. There will always be crazy individuals and no hundred per cent security, but I intend to get about just the same; to stay locked up here would be a wretched response. I will write to the Prime Minister and thank him for the police work on this sad case."

Julio was escorted out of the apartments, with a signed photo of Pope Peter to take home to his wife. He was wondering whether he ought to hunt Mr X in the Balkans, but soon realised that he would be totally ineffective looking for a single man in Serbia, Bosnia,

Montenegro, Kosovo, Macedonia, Albania, not knowing what ferry port had been used. The Pope was feeling well satisfied with the report and with the sweeping changes he was making to the Vatican staff. It was not that he wanted to replace conservatives with radicals, but rather ivory-towered clerics, wrapped in precedents, with people who understood the modern world. He had quickly appointed two laymen, one to be responsible for all travel arrangements and liaison with the church in countries to be visited, the other to look after the personnel office, all recruitment and service conditions. As he reviewed the departments, he transferred the Secretariat for Christian Unity under Terracini to become a desk in the office for International Affairs, clearly a demotion.

"You see," he told his new Secretary of State, "I am going to concentrate on our lapsed Catholics rather than on making friends with the other churches. We have five times the number of lapsed Catholics to those who are active in their faith. I want to draw them back. This means showing that we are truly in the great tradition of faith and that this faith speaks to modern fears and stresses. So I will certainly encourage the Reconciliation Council with the Orthodox to continue but I will not be rushing any reform that it suggests. I will let it mature and percolate. If it looks acceptable to our theologians then I will move."

So, at a stroke, Peter set back the ecumenical progress of Gregory, dismayed the adventurous, and affirmed the ancient stance that church unity meant "Come back to Mother."

***

It was an opposite tack in Kremlin affairs that brought on critical politics. The ascent of Ivan Markovic was a relief to all liberals, for it meant their first opportunity to publish a wide variety of views and speak more openly of their hopes for the future of their country. The grip of the Party was slackening; it no longer carried conviction, so although it was still there in the seats of power, it was as dummies, as a Madame Tussauds of wax, parading under the old red banner. But this relaxation was taken by some in quite another spirit. In the

Caucasus region, the bitterly divided communities saw the chance to raise a new flag, to press for their autonomy and then their independence, for their peoples had, through a long experience, no trust whatever in the rule of the Kremlin. In Eastern Europe, nations with a proud history could not any longer bear the rumble of Russian tanks and the Starsi knock on the door at midnight.

Markovic travelled extensively, meeting local leaders. His message was, it seemed, very practical. "It is not the central power that I come to represent here. I come to meet you and know you better. I come to see whether there may be a better relationship between us. So I do not come with tanks, and I have specifically asked the army commanders to give every respect to local organisations. But I want to urge you to think very carefully about what our relationship should be. It is not my role to destroy the Union. I would put it on a sounder basis, not the basis of military power but of consent. If I can work in Moscow to amend our system so as to enhance your freedom, I ask that you work here to think seriously on how best you can honour your traditions and hold a secure place in our Union.

I know this is not easy. There will be passions and extremists of all sorts. Do not be guided by them. You have learned and wise people, those with long experience and understanding. Let them become guides. But do not, for a moment, think that violence is going to win a victory; that is not the way. I will resist any violent movement just as any other breaking of the law. For we are a civilised people and we will show the world how to grow in freedom and responsibility. I call for your support. And I wish for you peace and prosperity."

This got a mixed reception in places as diverse as Hungary and Ukraine and Georgia. Nationalists of all sorts buckled on their armour, revised their speeches, drank beer with friends, published pamphlets and enlisted followers. It was also an opportunity for the Muslim peoples of the south of the Soviet empire to show their muscle, their majority, which had been quiescent too long. Some shoots of extremism sprouted from that old tree. Accidents happened to Soviet officials driving on lonely mountain roads. In Azerbaijan the production of oil mysteriously diminished. And in Tashkent the offices of the Party were firebombed. It could be held in check at first, but if it spread throughout the fringe of nationalities to the south and west of Russia, then it would be very hard to contain.

It was a path of risk for all, this attempt to liberalise a regime that had stood, with formidable power, for sixty years. Markovich could not see the end of it, the party faithful were gloomy and as uncommunicative as ever, and the army, the final bastion of orthodoxy, was losing its grip on the political system. As in many more primitive societies, Russians had a deep fear of chaos, that dark shadow of the forest, the sudden cry at midnight and the scramble for bread. Might not a severe, even a cruel regime save us? Perhaps democracy is a mistake.

Patriarch Minchov was well informed about the public mood. He reached out a hand of friendship to the President and wished him well, but understood that, if the system crumbled, then the Church would have to stand as the only firm and reliable institution in the nation. He could play a major role. As the Party dwindled, so the Church would rise, its song would be heard, and Russia would become Holy again. It would not be Church and State as political rivals, nor the Church as the private chaplain of those in power, but the Church as the soul in the body, the breath of the spirit and the wisdom of eternity, always present, the final home of all.

Neither the rising technocrats, nor the diverse nationalists, saw things in that frame, but they saw opportunity. Passports became easier to obtain and travel to the West no longer carried a heavy penalty. Foreign investment in Russian business began to increase, so that many of the old, inefficient heavy industries could at last adopt modern practice. The black market, which had been the petty criminals' route to stability, became the grey market, officially sanctioned and visited by Russians of all social origins. "It's all going too fast," many elderly people thought, "and will run off the rails."

In Britain, everyone was surprised by the resignation of the Prime Minister. He had won the general election, with a working majority in the House. There was much speculation on his decision, but it became clear that he was suffering from the first signs of dementia, had recognised this when his wife and doctor had spoken in plain terms, and then did the honest thing and resigned. It was one of the moments when the harsh realities of ageing became part of the national consciousness, a sign of the massive social problems of an ageing population. The demographic became part of the political conversation.

None of that concerned Niki and Elspeth. Happy with Katrina making a good start at the kindergarten on the Heworth road, within walking distance of their apartment, and busy with their own work, they could be optimistic in the run-up to Christmas. Elspeth planned for them to attend a performance of Handel's Messiah in York Minister.

"You think so much of Russian church music. It's time you heard some of ours. This should be good. Mum and Dad go every year, it's one of the traditions in many cities and shows off our choral singing at its best."

"Well, I'm not entirely ignorant, but I have never heard Handel's Messiah as a whole, just a few snatches. So this will be good education for me."

They found their seats in the great nave, the orchestra and choir placed in the crossing, and looked around at the splendid piers rising into the darkness, for the lighting expert had left the vaulted ceiling in shadow, the floodlights on the performers. Every seat was taken. The oratorio opened with gentleness and hope, rising to prophetic warnings and visions, bursting out in Hallelujahs. Then a pause. Niki was lost in the music and stayed still in his seat, impatient for the next part. This stirred him even more, with its depth of sorrow and ultimate victory. After the final Amen and then the applause, they walked hand-in-hand to their bus stop.

"Thank you, dear. That was a great experience. I must confess that my eyes were full of tears when that contralto sang 'He was despised and rejected'; it was the most perfect match of the text, the score and the voice. That was a musical revelation for me."

"For me too. I never get tired of it."

"I must listen to some more Handel. That kind of baroque is a total contrast to the Russian tradition. What else did he write?"

"I know he wrote a whole lot of operas, but I haven't seen any of them. Most of them were on classical themes. Some great songs.

Then there are suites and concertos, very easy to listen to. Dad has a number of recordings."

They were soon home, relieved the baby-sitter, who was one of Niki's students, and drank a toast to the music. In the year ahead Niki was to make a start on his next book, which was to be a historical and critical study of Church and State in Russia, starting with Vladimir at Kiev right up to the Communist supremacy, looking at how each side influenced the other.

Elspeth was making rapid progress on the series of discussion books for groups. She now had four completed texts – Niki on the Orthodox, the Archbishop of York on the Anglicans, Miriam Menzies on the Presbyterians and Walter Schwartz on the Lutherans. She ordered five hundred copies of each from the University Press, so that they could be used in promotions. The space in the crypt of Selby Abbey was now organised by her mother, with the help of a retired shopkeeper who was glad of a little extra to add to his pension. Her father had registered the private company as Demenchov Educational Services, with its bank account in the NatWest Bank. Elspeth posted explanatory notes about the whole series and the four booklets to the Education Officers of all the English Anglican and Catholic dioceses and to the head offices of the other main churches. She sent review copies to the religious papers and a copy to the Council of Churches in America, with a special commendation from Miriam. Then she paused. Would there be a response?

To the surprise of the family, the response was rapid and encouraging. The Tablet and the Church Times gave the series very favourable reviews. The Ecumenical Review, published by the World Council of Churches, gave a half page advertisement at very generous rates, and this went round the world. Ten of the Anglican dioceses sent orders, the Methodist Conference office was collecting responses from all the Districts and the Church of Scotland was delighted to see the text by Miriam Menzies. It looked as though the Selby office would need a secretary to keep the orders and accounts. The retired shopkeeper, George Wallace, who had started as a packer, soon found himself with a desk and a filing cabinet. Elspeth was fully occupied with finding the writers and editing their work, expanding the list within twelve months to sixteen Christian communions.

She had her eye on the American market. "Do you think, Niki, that I could go to America when the National Council of Churches is meeting, so that I could talk to the key people in the major churches?"

"That's a big thing to attempt, dear. Do you really feel ready for that?"

"Yes, I think we have to see just how big this enterprise can be. It could be a single firework and then die down. I want to find out if there is a future in this sort of publishing."

"Then you must follow your intention. I won't hold you back at all. But I want to be in touch with you even if you are far away. Katrina would miss you terribly. Could you make it a short trip?"

"Yes. My contact in Philadelphia says that the meeting lasts four days, so if I had a week I could visit a few of the church headquarters as well."

Two months later she was on her way. A box of sample material had been sent on by sea. Elspeth flew to New York and then on to Pittsburgh where the meeting was held in the large Presbyterian Seminary campus. She had a stall in the Market Place, where there was much competition for attention, with all the major religious publishers, the youth organisations, the civil rights campaigners and the Holy Land travel agencies all displaying their wares. Elspeth found that she needed to close her stall early so that she was free to wander around the auditorium, meeting staff members of the churches. The sheer energy, diversity, numbers and enterprise stimulated and rather frightened her. She felt like the country cousin suddenly in the metropolis. She had one immediate success, with the President of the United Church of Christ, which had its main strength in New England, for he at once saw an ideal vehicle to promote his own drive to widen the influence of ecumenism during his term of office; he would ensure an order for a hundred sets. The Episcopalians were so occupied with their internal debate over women bishops and the risks of schism that it was hard to interest their people. The Reformed Church, with its German influences, seemed ready to take the matter to its education department, and the Disciples, from their

Indianapolis headquarters, were enthusiastic, immediately ordering fifty sets to send to the senior minister in each of the States

It was an exhausting week. Elspeth slept in her seat as she flew back across the Atlantic. "Yes, Niki, it was well worth the cost. There are some big orders to be mailed and I expect some more to come within a month or so, when the various committees have churned over the sets I left with them."

"Then you will have to order another printing, for the first lot have mostly gone."

"That's fine, so long as we have the income in the bank. But it's big business there, and lots of competition from the publishers. I think we ought to appoint an agency there to handle advertising and ordering. The church people would find it easier to deal with an American than with us here. I got to know the manager of a small publishing firm, Fortitude Press, in Boston. He publishes new church music and books of prayers and some commentaries. I wonder if that could become our agent. He would have to receive a share of the selling price, but I think it might be well worth it. Could we have a chat with someone you know at the University Press to see if the idea would float?"

"You are running ahead of me, dear, but yes, we could do that very easily." He could see that she was on the upswing of a career, something fully consuming of her thoughts and talents. There was already talk of a German translation of the series. Where would it end? He felt that in some inevitable way she was moving on a different track while he stayed quietly teaching and caring for Katrina. It was not jealousy of her success, for he rejoiced that such a piece of work could be their combined offering, but the fear of a distance between them. Was it wrong to want her close and warm and confiding and at home? Perhaps his Russian culture had left a paterfamilias imprint on his character.

In the crypt at Selby there were now two permanent workers, the packer and George, the secretary. The company was paying the abbey rent for the space, always welcome to the budget. Orders were arriving by every mail, often for small items, just one course or two, for local groups. The bank account looked healthy. Three months after her

American trip, a letter arrived for Elspeth from a lawyer in Atlanta, Georgia. It stated that his client, Lighthouse Publications Pty Ltd, sought the immediate stop of all sales of the Meet the Family series or else she would meet the challenge of infringement of copyright in the courts.

Totally dismayed, her stomach churning, she rushed to the phone to speak with her father. She read the letter to him. "What should I do, Dad? I can't stop sales because we have dispatched large orders to America and they have been paid for. Business is going so well."

"I think, dear, that the first thing to do is for me, as your solicitor, to write back saying that their letter is having our most careful consideration and will be responded to as quickly as possible. The next thing is for you to phone one of your best contacts in America to get a copy of any material that Lighthouse has published that looks anything at all like ours, and to post that to you by airmail. Then we will know whether it is a genuine challenge or not."

"Thanks, Dad. You are terrific. Tonight I will phone Philadelphia. They will know what sort of firm this is in Atlanta. I don't think anyone had done a series like ours, but we shall soon see."

The news from Philadelphia was that this company was a small publisher, not primarily of religious material, but of do-it-yourself books. They would post specimens of the series on the churches, which seemed to be called The Christian World Series; it was not widely known. When the packet arrived, Elspeth was immediately reassured, for the booklets did not look like hers. They did cover much of the same ground, each booklet on a denomination, the list of topics very similar, but each was 12 to 20 pages, designed for individual readers, and with no special attention to group discussion, though some of them had questions at the end. She drove to Selby in the little second-hand car they had bought, taking the material to her father's office and they discussed it together.

"Dad, it looks so different. Of course there is material which is similar because it is historical, describing how the churches came to be formed as they are. But it is not the same language at all. Our writers haven't copied anything. And our format is different, with the single session parts and the discussion materials and the pictures, maps and timelines. Surely there can't be a question of copyright."

"I think that is so. It does seem a very different style of material for a different readership. I think they are trying it on, perhaps seeing us as amateurs and easily shaken. It could be that they don't like an English newcomer in the American market. I think we should reply that we have inspected their material and see no reason why copyright should be at issue, and so challenge them to proceed if they wish, knowing that the case will be fought. We would then have to engage an American law firm, and that would be expensive. Can we do that?"

"I think we will have to. Look, here is our latest bank statement. What do you think?"

"It might make a big hole in this, but I agree that you cannot stop the sales and the income because of a threat like this."

"I'll see if Niki has any ideas."

That evening Niki was disturbed at the news – the very idea of a legal challenge in the US seemed a major obstacle. Russians did not go to the courts with the ease of Americans. But he had an idea.

"When I was at the Moscow seminary, one of the teachers was an expert of church law and admin. He went on to become the Chancellor, or the legal advisor, to the Orthodox bishop in New York. I'm sure he would be able to advise us on the way forward there. I'll call Moscow and find out if he is still there and what his phone number is. I can explain that we do not have much to spend."

The result was that a firm of sympathetic lawyers was engaged, so that when the court summons arrived, Francis Beach was able to refer it to the firm of Dean Dilman Zanuch at their good New York address, saying that the action would be defended, and sending the Meet the Family series so they could compare the material. The preliminary hearing was scheduled for two months ahead.

At that stage Elspeth and Niki were not needed in court, so were represented by John Zanuch in the case of Lighthouse Publications v. Demenchov Educational Services. The Atlanta people based their case on the fact that their series of booklets went onto the market at the same time as the British series arrived in America, that they covered the same ground, their lists of subjects were almost identical, and that the treatment in several of the booklets looked very similar.

"Here we have a case, Your Honour, of an opportunistic foreign firm coming into the market place in direct competition with our publication which has been in preparation for two years. It is a copy-cat enterprise and should be stopped."

The defence made a strong argument; John Zanuch was well briefed. "Here are two series, planned independently, written by different authors, and intended for different purposes. You see that the Lighthouse series has texts of 12 to 20 pages, quite a serious essay on each religious body, presumably intended for serious readers and students. The Meet the Family series is expressly designed for small group discussion. The text runs to only four pages, there are two pages of discussion material and two pages of pictures and diagrams. There is no pretence that these are for serious students but for ordinary church members who are broadening their horizon. In no case has the actual text been taken from the Lighthouse series. There is no plagiarism. It is plain that if there are two attempts to write about the Lutheran Reformation, for example, then much of that material will be similar. It could not be otherwise; it is a historical event, but it is surely ridiculous to suggest that only one person can write about it. We can only see this as an attempt to stifle competition and ask that the case be dismissed."

The judge retired to read the booklets more carefully. She returned to court an hour later.

"I have come to the conclusion that this matter should not proceed to the district court. The only close similarity here is the scope of the two series. There is no infringement of copyright or of intellectual property, since no material has been copied from one to the other. There must be freedom to publish what is separately designed and written and distributed. Suppose there are two or three series of books on the artists of the Italian Renaissance – which there surely are – you cannot suppress two of them in order to give the third a sole privilege to publish. That would be an illegal restraint on trade. There is plenty of room in this great market place of the USA for two series on the churches to flourish for they will appeal to different constituencies. I can see the Lighthouse series being very helpful to students of comparative religion and the history of religion, while Meet the Family would be right for house groups in all the churches. The case is dismissed and legal costs are awarded to the defendents."

It was a clear win. In Yorkshire a dark cloud was lifted. Elspeth and Niki thought a day out was in order and drove with Katrina to Sewerby on the coast near Bridlington to see the fine old house, now a museum, with llamas in the garden and a splendid old monkey puzzle tree. Fish and chips for lunch, sunshine on the sea and the old Ford performing well; it meant a modest celebration for them all.

***

For Patriarch Minchov, as for most thoughtful Russians, there was a conflict between his hopes for reform and his fears for nationalist and religious violence. He respected Ivan Markovich as a President with ideas, not at all the dead wood of the Party, but he wondered whether military and police action could hold the network of nationalities together. Many would suffer. He had no admiration for the Moslem enthusiasts in the south who were welding together their faith, their politics and their tradition of militancy. But then, he thought, who am I to criticise those who hold church and state to be close partners. As for Eastern Europe, let them go! They were ancient nations with strong identities and could not be subject to the Russian grip for ever. The test for Markovich would be whether as independent states they could regard Russia as a friend across the borders. If not, if they turned to the West, it would be the old story of tension and suspicion.

Serious fighting started in the Caucasus, country ideal for guerrilla bands intimate with the mountain paths and hopeless for the Russian heavy weapons. First in Grozny, then south in the hills and spreading to Georgia, Russian convoys were ambushed, military outposts overwhelmed and the stability of the regime threatened. Then, on one March day, the wind cutting like ice from the mountains, a van backed into the loading bay of the municipal office block on the main square of Grozny, delivering some desks and chairs. It was a six storey building, housing 150 staff. As the van driver opened the back door of the van, there was a mighty crump, a blast that shook every building around, a bang that could be heard twenty kilometres away, and the air was thick with dust and smoke. The whole rear wall of the block collapsed. Every floor started to tilt dangerously. Furniture and members of staff were cascading onto rubble. Splinters of glass sliced through clothing and flesh. The cries of the wounded were hardly heard after the concussion of the blast.

The rescue teams, ambulances and fire appliances soon appeared, blocking all the streets, and as the dust began to settle they were able to estimate the crisis. Indiscriminately the dead and wounded were gathered, covered with blankets, put into ambulances and moved to the two main hospitals, their emergency rooms soon overflowing. For the next two days the mountain of rubble was pulled apart, several people found alive, but more were dead.

Chechnya had told Moscow, You have a fight on your hands, and the blood is on your hands too if you refuse our independence. Even a liberally-minded President could not ignore this challenge. The army was called into full action and hundreds of suspects brought into temporary lock-ups. Their chances of a fair trial were remote, for the fury of the authorities had to be expressed and their power publicly seen.

"I hate what I am forced to do," he told his cabinet, "but there is no option. We cannot allow the whole Soviet Union to give in to such savagery."

It became a long, messy campaign, leading nowhere. Many utility coffins arrived at city railway stations across Russia, to be met by wailing relatives. Priests received them with honour. Then, on another front, there was a series of labour strikes in Poland organised by the Solidarity movement, which showed it had widespread support. Workers against a socialist government – what kind of orthodoxy is this? In Czechoslovakia it was the literary and artistic set which moved popular feeling, with satire the main weapon of the day, performers on the streets of Prague singing national songs and guying the abject series of Russian Presidents. When the police appeared the actors immediately became clowns doing their tricks.

In his grand Moscow office, Markovich no longer had confidence in himself. He knew his decent record, there was no corruption to be ashamed of, but he was finding his very real limitations and wore a look of perpetual dismay. Patriarch Minchov was saddened by events, looking towards the break-up of the Union with no pleasure at all, and longing for some good news, some stability in the life of the Church. Perhaps that was the only ground on which to stand, the City of God, in Augustine's language, when the City of Mankind was in disarray.

***

Near the town of Tarquinia, some 75 kilometres north of Rome, Professor Craxi was contentedly poking around yet another Etruscan tomb. He was the king of archaeologists at the Milan City University and had directed a team of students, clearing a site of several mounds of earth and stones which covered the ancient burial chambers. The Etruscans were mysterious. Pre-Roman, their relics were found mainly in Perugia and Terni, and were limited to clay statues and some rural implements, and the many grave sites which had been uncovered and robbed over centuries. Craxi was confirming the latest tomb in the afternoon after the students had left and the watchman was lazily setting up his shelter for the night. In this tomb the accumulation of soil filled the bottom half of the vault, but with a torch he could see the upper walls and the roofing. He was struck by a cavity in a wall near the roof, properly clad in stone, as though a niche to be filled with an important skeleton. There were no bones there that he could see. Instead there was a block of very solid material, the size of a paving stone.

He reached out to see if it was moveable. As he gripped the edge of the block, it cracked and the hard covering of that corner fell away. Shining his torch on that corner he could see what looked like frayed tatters of cloth around skin or hides. Carefully he tapped around the edges, and more of the hard shell cracked away. It was the accumulation of dirt and dust of a millennium. He saw that in this tomb there seemed to be an ancient codex, a parchment book, which he could lift. He walked quickly back to his car, opened the boot and took out a strong groundsheet, which the family used at picnic lunches, and took this back to the tomb. Then, at full stretch (and he was not a big man) he drew the codex out of the cavity and laid it on the sheet, wrapping it as well as he could. Well aware that this was all irregular and that he should have waited for the team to come next morning to document the find, he considered his authority sufficient to ignore the rules.

He drove to Viterbo, joined the autostrada, and made good speed north, the traffic was light and his Fiat running smoothly. It was midnight when he reached home and locked the car into the underground garage. He could hardly sleep, his wife saying in a pained voice, "Take a pill if you can't sleep."

Next morning Craxi drove to the university, where he had a reserved parking place. He went into the main laboratory of the department to meet his senior archaeological staff, two long-serving colleagues whose expertise he could trust.

"I am doing something rather unusual which I need you to keep confidential. I assure you it is necessary. I want to bring in a parcel from the car. It is a bundle which I found in tomb C134 at Tarquinia and which I think may be a valuable find. Treat it with great care. Don't involve other people. We will slowly separate some layers of material, preserving every scrap."

He also phoned instructions to the senior student on the site at Tarquinia. "This is Craxi here. I have removed a bundle from C134. I need you to make a detailed survey of the vault, with special attention to the cavity near the ceiling. Please make a careful photo record of this. You will see the space on the floor of that cavity, a rectangle, where the bundle was. Measure it accurately. I have removed the object for special analysis here in the lab. Do you understand?"

Work in the lab was painstaking but exciting. The two women staff, tutors with strong academic records, removed the shreds and tatters of cloth around the bundle, taking photos at every stage, and revealed a codex, the bound vellum pages of an ancient text. The top page showed unmistakable old Greek uncial letters.

"Let's pause here," Craxi said, "and think what we have. A costly manuscript, wrapped up and hidden in an Etruscan tomb. That's not how a wealthy owner would treat his treasure. It might be how a fugitive or a thief would hide something of value while he was being chased. Or it could be a deposit in a place of comparative safety when the owners were in big trouble. The text will tell us which is most likely, but no jumping to conclusions!"

The writing on the first sheet was faded, but they could just make out "Euangellion…Iesu ", Gospel of Jesus. The second sheet and all the others were much clearer, and had been well protected from the dirt and dust of the ages. They revealed a Gospel which was indeed the Gospel of Mark. An early Mark. Perhaps very old. Surely very precious. From the number of sheets it looked as though it was a complete Gospel, but it would need a biblical scholar to check that.

"Let us keep this under wraps until we have some more certainty about it. I will have to decide on the next steps and don't want to be rushed. Let us put it in a metal box and I will deposit it in the archive strong room. The humidity there is well controlled."

Craxi was not an expert on Greek manuscripts, so realised that there would have to be referral to others, and it was a matter of great importance to choose the right people. First, to fix the dating, he would need the best carbon dating labs, and considered that Oxford, Chicago and Paris would be totally reliable. So samples of the fibre covering material and the vellum itself would have to be sent and tested; that would take time. But then he needed to consider that the writing might not be of the same date. So he needed a second set of experts in the writing of Greek manuscripts in Italy. For this he chose the Vatican archive centre, the Hebrew University in Jerusalem and the Berlin museum of the Greek and Roman world. They would all need very good photos of several pages, chosen at random.

There was a month before any response could be expected and Craxi found it hard to remain silent on his find. It was the number of fakes on the market that made him particularly cautious; to go public on an important find and then to be taken down and exposed as a gullible fool – that would not do for a senior professor in Milan. So he tried to be busy about other things. There were enough internal politics in the university to keep staff hectically attending meetings, and always post-graduate students to guide and encourage.

Then results trickled in, with no wide variations. The carbon dating showed that the material was dated between 250 and 300 AD. Chicago put it close to 250, Oxford and Paris in the 270 to 300 range. The writing experts gave much the same figure. The Berlin expert stated that the writing was not that of a highly trained scholar but of well-educated clerk or similar. They all agreed on a pre-300 date.

Craxi knew that the earliest full text of the Gospels that was known, the Codex Sinaiaticus in the British Museum, was dated about 100 years later than this. He was now confident that they had in their hands a treasure of immense value, the oldest written Gospel known. He needed to share his excitement. He called Cardinal Terracini, whom he had met at university ceremonies, and made an appointment, taking with him a full photographic copy of the text.

"I need to share with you, with all your biblical knowledge, a wonderful find we have made in our archaeological work. It was in an Etruscan tomb at Tarquinia and has been uncovered and cared for in my confidential lab at the university. It is a Greek manuscript on vellum and is a Gospel of Mark. I have had it checked for its dating in three expert carbon dating labs and the writing confirmed by three specialist Greek scholars. All are agreed that this codex dates from 250 to 300 AD, and so is the oldest written Gospel ever found. Here is a photo copy of the entire text."

"My dear Craxi, this is a very great discovery. This will draw scholars from all over the world. We shall need to think about how to deal with it, but first may I look at some of these pages?"

He looked at the first two pages, and translated them as he went. It was the very same wording that he had come to know by heart, the opening of the Gospel of Mark. He then turned to the ending, knowing that this was a highly debated matter. In the best manuscripts the Gospel ended with a very abrupt and unconvincing verse: *Then the women went out and ran away from the tomb, trembling with amazement. They said nothing to anyone, for they were afraid.* That did not real like the ending of the story, and several alternatives had been found, of later dates. But here, Tarracini saw, was a different ending, in fact a whole page of material he had never seen before. It recorded the appearing of Jesus to the twelve and then to a crowd of five hundred people at the Mount of Olives.

"This is wonderful. Here must be the last page which somehow was lost from all the other copies. In those difficult days, how easy it must have been to lose the last sheet of the codex, and then all the scribes later on would have no knowledge of it. This page alone makes this manuscript fundamental to all Bible scholars. I need to sit down for a bit and think about it. You are sure of the dating?"

"Certainly, I could not have found better expertise anywhere."

"That means that this is before Constantine, before Jerome. Just let me look at the emperors. Yes, there was Domitian who ruled from 280. He was a persecutor of Christians. Could it be that some Christians left Rome, with this document, to escape to the country, and there found new trouble, so hid their precious Gospel? We can't prove that but it seems to me a reasonable supposition."

They sat talking for an hour. They agreed that there would need to be a public announcement and a ceremonial revealing of the contents. They saw the need to work together, university and church, to carry this through with appropriate dignity. Then the question is bound to arise, they realised, about where such a treasure would be permanently lodged, but they did not arrive at an answer.

The Cardinal took on the arrangements for the public ceremony, which he saw as an opportunity for bringing together a large number of church leaders and scholars. Milan Cathedral would be the place for it. Next day he started writing the invitation list, headed by the Pope. He wrote the invitation in compelling terms.

On the 18th of September 1990 we shall be unveiling to the public the greatest Biblical discovery of our era, a text of the Gospel of Mark from the Third Century, brought to light by the Archaeology Department of the University of Milan. This well-attested Codex sets a new standard for the text, and has some surprises. It is the oldest text of a complete Gospel extant.

We ask you to accept this invitation to be present at Milan Cathedral at 12 noon on that date to share in this event, which has great importance for the universal church.

The Cardinal wrote a personal letter to the Pope with this printed invitation, assuring him that devotion to the Gospel made this a high priority, giving him a hint that the true ending of Mark had been found. He had already learned from the Pope's secretary that the date would be possible in the papal diary. The invitation went to the Patriarch in Moscow, to several of the Cardinals, to the Anglican leaders and many others. It would be very major gathering. Special seating at the cathedral and good lighting would be in the hands of the experienced maintenance staff. The press and TV would be managed, he hoped, by the Public Relations office of the university.

In Moscow the invitation brought a sense of relief to the Patriarch, who was longing to escape from the bitterness of the political conflicts which were infecting all public life. Yes, he would go and take a party of senior Orthodox. The Metropolitan from Constantinople and the Archbishop from Kiev and his personal scholarly friends – they would make a good presence in that famous cathedral. And the Syrian Orthodox ought to be there too.

In Canterbury and York there was some puzzled conversation. Why Milan? Why not in Rome? But September in Italy was no bad thing. What could be the surprise in the text? If the Pope was attending then certainly they should both be there, with Anglicans from the five continents to show how global the communion was. In India the elderly bishop of the Mar Toma church, the guardian of a tradition going back to the apostolate of Thomas, saw a rare opportunity to share in a world event. The Geneva response was immediate, Yes, the World Council must be there to embrace a Biblical reality. Even the Southern Baptists in the US found it hard to resist, suspicious as they were of Catholic enticements, for the Bible was the absolute foundation of their faith.

When it became public that the Pope would be attending, the city authorities joined the party with offers of security staff. They suggested that, after the cathedral service, there should be an al fresco lunch in the piazza for 250 guests, seated at round tables, the city providing the meal. Terracini thought this was a splendid idea but feared bad weather. "What?" said the mayor, "You doubt your own prayers? It will be great weather."

So it was. By 11.0 the cathedral was well filled, the delegations in special seating surrounding the crossing. The stewards had never been so challenged to acknowledge the variety of Christian leaders, but retained their sense of good order. The organ music rolled around the heavy columns. Niki and Elspeth were tucked in behind the Anglican Archbishops, and, as he looked round, Niki realised that he could have been equally at home in the Orthodox or the Catholic section. Then Pope Peter and his entourage processed, the crowd standing, the trumpet stop on the organ on forte. There was a pause while the congregation settled; then Terracini and Craxi came forward to lead the programme.

The Cardinal welcomed the congregation. "We are gathered here to witness a remarkable discovery, to hear the precious word of God, and to give thanks for the message of life that it brings to us. I want to express the appreciation of the Church to the University of Milan and expressly to Professor Craxi, who has been the principal scholar concerned with this discovery, but who has renounced any personal benefit, so that this text of the Gospel may be readily available to all. I now ask him to tell us all how this Gospel was discovered and authenticated."

"Your Holiness and all honoured guests, I usually give my lectures to students and now find myself speaking to my seniors, so please excuse me if I fail to do justice to your expertise and devotion. This story begins with ancient Etruscan tombs. That may sound a very dull subject. But my Department has been at work for years to try to put together a more cohesive picture of the life of those ancient people. Six months ago I was inspecting a tomb that we had just uncovered; it seemed the usual sort of thing, nothing special. But I noted that in the cavity there was a niche or shelf high up near the roof, with a block of stone in it. I was looking for bones, but there were none. I pulled the corner of the stone and it crumbled in my hand. I found that it was a crust of dirt covering a bundle that I could manipulate out of the niche. This was very unusual. It was too delicate to deal with on site. It was recorded and I took it personally from the site at Tarquinia to the laboratory of the Department here in Milan. It was treated with the greatest care and unwrapped, so revealing a vellum codex. My first inspection showed me that it was a Greek text of the Gospel of Mark. I am not a Biblical expert so I did not attempt to read it all. But it was clearly an early text. We needed to know something of its origin.

I therefore asked experts to provide opinions of its age. Carbon dating of the wrapping and the vellum was done at Oxford, Chicago and Paris, and dating of the writing was confirmed by the Vatican archive centre, the Hebrew University in Jerusalem and the Berlin Museum of Greek and Roman Antiquities. All these six reports came to us with a unanimous verdict, that this text comes from the period between 250 and 300 AD. It is thus by far the oldest full text of a Gospel ever found. We can make many surmises about how it came to be lodged in an Etruscan tomb, but have no evidence to affirm that.

My work was really finished at that point, so I shared the text with my friend the Cardinal, who at once realised how this text varies from what we have received before. Just as Tischendorf set a new standard by his discovery at Sinai, so Tarquinia brings us a fresh light on the Gospel of Mark."

The choir then sang a psalm, 'The word of the Lord is more precious than gold.' The congregation stood for the Procession of the Word. Down the long central aisle came a verger leading a small group in the spotlights, four teenage girls in white holding staffs, each crowned with the lion of St Mark, escorting a Franciscan monk, a tall, plain, thin figure holding aloft in both hands the precious codex. This was placed reverently on the central altar. The Cardinal announced, "At this point we are not going to read the whole text of the Gospel. There are many very small variations here from the received text, but only one major change. That is the ending of the Gospel. We are reading the newly revealed ending of Mark. The stewards are now distributing to you all a print of this ending in its Greek, but also translated into Latin, English, French and Russian so that you all may hear the word."

A pause followed as the stewards passed the leaflets around to all the two thousand congregation. Then a young priest, with a clear, deep voice read:

Later that day Jesus appeared to the disciples in the upper room, saying, 'Peace be with you. You see that I am with you now and I will be with you always. Follow my way and keep my word.'

On the next Sabbath he appeared on the road out of the city to the Mount of Olives, followed by a crowd of five hundred people from Jerusalem. Many of the poor and the sick from the city were there. Jesus laid hands on many of the sick and healed them.

Then, looking towards the city, he said, 'I have spoken truth that the walls of the temple will fall in ruin and the people will flee. Do not be dismayed. The way of worship by making sacrifices on those altars is now finished and you will worship God in spirit and in truth. Wherever you go, your lives will be your prayer. As you forgive those who sin against you, care for the sick and visit those in prison, and as you love one another, so your heavenly Father is worshipped and glorified. You will be as priests, each in your own home.

Be of one mind as you follow my way. There will always be wolves seeking to scatter the flock. Do not let the powers of this world lead you away from the truth, but let the Spirit hold you fast to my teaching. All who follow me are one as children of the Father in the one household of faith.

You see and know today that death is overcome by life. Life now and life for ever is the gift of the Father. You live always in the presence of God.'

With these words he blessed them and disappeared from their sight. The crowd praised God for the wonderful things they had seen and heard.

The congregation was silent for several minutes. Then the Pope stood and led in prayer, "Heavenly Father, we who hear your word seek to learn and to follow the way revealed to us in Jesus Christ. By your grace and mercy, and with all the saints, may we be faithful all the days of our lives, even to death, and beyond death, in the light of your presence. Amen. We now say the Lord's Prayer, each in his own language"

This was followed by a burst of Palestrina on the organ. Terracini and Craxi, with the leaders of the major communions, moved with the Pope to a vestry and slowly the delegations moved out to dazzling sunshine in the piazza. The invited guests went to the tables, shaded by big white market umbrellas, to enjoy a variety of salads, cold meats, and chicken, followed by the splendid new crop of peaches, nectarines and grapes, and a selection of the best Italian cheeses. The chatter was constant. "What a discovery! And what a final chapter. So Paul was right in saying that Jesus appeared to five hundred at one time. Did you get the message about priests? What can that mean for the church?" Elspeth and Niki found the group from Geneva; Elspeth and Miriam embraced, godmother and daughter in spirit. "Now there is something we must study and broadcast, for it sounds like an ecumenical voice. Do you think it is really going to be in the new Bibles?" The Vatican party saw the Pope off in his helicopter and then enjoyed the meal.

Terracini was everywhere, greeting old friends and making new ones. He found Niki and embraced him as a colleague. "You are the very best note-taker and minute-writer, so I am sure you have a note on this gathering. Show me."

"I was too moved by it to write much, just a couple of lines when the organ was playing.

Gathered to hear the word of the Lord, for this hour the church was one.

That's all I felt I could write. There is much more to think about for days to come."

"You are right, Nikolas, I don't think there has ever been such a united presence of the church. So after our disappointments, perhaps our false expectations, something has happened which will change the future.'

"There is one item which puzzles me. Where do you intend this treasure to find a home? A University Department here hardly seems fitting."

"That has been worrying me. I don't want it to be identified with one of the communions, so that rules out the Vatican. I've thought of the British Museum, to go alongside the Sinaiaticus. Or the Library of Congress, where the professional care is matchless. But my decision, subject to the wishes of the University, is to put it into the care of the

Franciscans in Assisi. That is an international shrine and is close to the area where the Codex was found. I believe that they would give it the best balance of exposure and security possible in central Italy. And we could insist that it was not to be a money-making display but free for all, though obviously kept safely behind glass. What do you think?"

"That sounds good to me. I have to thank you for the way you have handled this explosion of interest and for all your leadership through the years. You have been one of my best guides. Your meals are pretty good, too!"

With Elspeth, he wandered to the Russian group, who were clearing the plates at their table and seemed ready to fill bags with the fruit. "Did you hear that, Niki? We're all priests now."

"Well, that ties in with the letter of Peter, and if Peter's preaching lies behind Mark, then it's not so surprising. But certainly it makes us all review what we have always thought about the priesthood."

"What a pity you married. You would have made a fine bishop!"

"Please, don't say that. Elspeth here might have second thoughts about me. She took a big risk with a deacon."

Then, with the municipal band playing airs from Puccini, the groups filtered out of the piazza, many of them lingering in the Galleries and strolling to the central station, its grandiose spaces a second cathedral. Niki and Elspeth caught the local train from the Garibaldi station to Malpensa airport. In the airport lounge, they talked over the day.

"I think that I have learned something worthwhile, dear. You see, much of my life I have worked on the theme of bringing people together, people from all the churches, so that they could come to a new understanding, a new face for the church. That was not a bad theme. I'm sure it is one of the keys to friendship and true fellowship. But it is not enough. People can meet together and then drift apart as though nothing has happened. They are not changed at a deep enough level. That's true of me too.

I see now that it when we all face a new challenge that we become one. A family or a nation may have many differences among the members, many arguments, but it is when they all together face some new challenge, some disaster or war or a great opportunity, that they become united.

Here today this is what was happening. All the thousand different understandings and habits of mind and cultural settings, all the titles and authorities, all were confronted by another voice, a voice from the beyond. That's the real key. That's how the big shift in church history will come. And that's really what the whole incarnation tells us, Listen to the voice from beyond. It may be the voice of a great prophet or perhaps the cries during a disaster or maybe some wonderful music. Today it was that ancient voice, that Jerusalem mystery, but through it we heard the echo of creation and life."

"Darling, you are getting eloquent, you're preaching. Let's just get home and climb down from the mountain."

***

Printed in Great Britain
by Amazon